Royally Engaged

By
Jill Boyce

Editor: Cynthia Hickey
Book Design by Forget Me Not Romances

ISBN 978-1-0879-6740-0

"I am the vine; you are the branches. If you remain in me and I in you, you will bear much fruit; apart from me you can do nothing." John 15:5 (NIV)

Prologue

Claire Thomson stared at the engagement ring on her left hand. She twisted it between her thumb and first finger of her right hand, sliding the ring up and down. Pulling it off, she glanced at her naked finger where the ring had resided. Shifting her eyes, she looked over the lake next to Evercliff Castle.

Claire let her gaze settle on the crystal blue water spotted with green lily pads topped with white flowers. Would the wedding happen?

Storm clouds gathered overhead, and the wind kicked up, carrying the scent of impending rain with it. The sky darkened, and the weight of the cumulus clouds mirrored the heaviness Claire carried on her shoulders. A loud crack of lightning reverberated through the air, interrupting her thoughts. Claire rose and dusted bits of grass off her linen skirt.

"Come on, Wilson," she called to her golden retriever puppy, "let's go."

He stood and grabbed a stick he'd found. The piece of wood twice his size hung out both sides of his mouth, but it couldn't hide his grin.

Planting her hands on her hips, Claire tilted her head. "You look pretty pleased with yourself. I don't know how you're going to carry that back to the castle—not to mention that there's no way Albert's going to let you through the door with it."

1

The puppy's jaw tightened around the stick.

She shook her head. "Okay, you can bring it with you, but don't blame me if Albert takes it away from you." She headed toward the castle as tiny raindrops fell from the sky. She had so much to do and not enough time to accomplish everything—the wedding, the coronation, and her medical responsibilities.

Reviewing her to-do list made Claire's head spin. She drew in a deep breath. Could she handle it? She'd have to—she had no choice. Besides, Mona Thomson had drilled one thing into her daughter's mind, "Nothing ever gets done if you don't do it yourself." That, and, "You can rest when you're dead." Claire had one option—to pull herself together and make it happen. She couldn't consider the alternative. Especially not with Maurelle lurking in the wings.

A small sob escaped Claire's lips, but she tamped it down. The rain intensified, pelting Claire's face with sharp, cold droplets. Clenching her eyes, Claire wiped away the wetness. She couldn't tell where the storm's precipitation ended, and her tears began.

"Hurry, Wilson." She waved to the puppy and pried the stick from his mouth. Then, she scooped him into her arms and ran the rest of the way to the castle. Her legs burned, screaming in protest at the spontaneous activity. Claire tightened her jaw. She couldn't quit, couldn't rest, couldn't fail. No—she'd somehow find a way to handle it all. Somehow.

Chapter 1
May

Claire spun around, her eyes searching desperately for the book that ran her life—her planner. She didn't maintain organization in many arenas—cooking, housekeeping, or just about any other domestic duty. However, when it came to her schedule and professional obligations, Claire prided herself on keeping a detailed schedule. She'd never missed a dental appointment, work deadline, or a mail hold. Never—until now.

She sighed and rubbed her hand across her forehead. Closing her eyes, she willed her memory to bring into view the last location of the beloved itinerary keeper. Nothing. Nada.

A hand settled on Claire's shoulder.

She jumped, startled by the unexpected touch. Gasping, Claire whipped around and found the culprit. "Granny, you nearly gave me a heart attack. Don't sneak up on me like that. Give a grumble or clear your throat—something."

A teasing twinkle appeared in Granny's eyes. "Where would the fun be in that? Then, you wouldn't have gasped and made that face. You looked like Old

3

Lady Pearl after I won the final game of Bingo last summer. Boy did that surprise her—her mouth hung open like a cod." Granny smacker her hand on her knee and guffawed. "Oh, I loved it."

Claire found her breath again and chastised her granny, "That's not nice. You know Pearl is not well. You shouldn't be glad that you shocked her."

Granny scrunched her nose and crossed her arms in front of her chest. "Pshaw. She's fine. She's not that old—no older than me. You won't let me have any fun. What's gotten you worked into a tizzy?"

Scanning the room again, Claire prayed the book might appear suddenly on the desk in her bedroom—as if it'd been there all along and she'd simply overlooked it. Nope. "I'm trying to find my planner. It has everything in it—my clinic and surgical schedule, ideas I had for the hospital's charity, and a to-do list from the queen mother for Coronation Day. That's the one I'm most upset about because she already thinks I don't take this royal stuff seriously. If I tell her I've forgotten all the things she wanted me to do for the coronation, it's going to reinforce this belief." Claire paced back and forth across the room, chewing on her thumbnail, trying to think.

Granny stepped forward, blocking her path. "Listen here, Missy. You need to calm down. Rest. You know what that word means, right?"

Claire pressed her lips together. "Of course, I do. I don't have time for rest."

Granny narrowed her eyes. "Well, you'd better make time. You know what the Bible says about the importance of rest, don't you?"

Claire sighed but humored her granny. "What?"

"It says that you can't do anything on your own. If you try to handle all this stuff by yourself, then you're going to get rotten apples."

Raising a brow, Claire lifted her eyes to meet Granny's. "Rotten apples?"

Granny gave a firm nod. "Rotten apples. Bad fruit. Look it up—you'll see. I'm telling you the truth. You can't do all this on your own."

Claire didn't have time for nursery stories today. "Thanks, but right now, I can't worry about my fruit going bad. I've got to find that planner."

Granny opened her mouth, probably ready to give another cent or two about how Claire should live life. A knock on the door interrupted her monologue.

Claire's shoulders relaxed. "Come in," she called, thankful for a break in the lecture series from Granny.

Ethan Kane, Claire's dashing fiancé, former Earl of Abbingdon, and swoon-worthy Christian gentleman extraordinaire, opened the door and stuck his head through the crack.

A smile flew to her lips, and immediately her worries lightened. Ethan always had that effect on her. He made everything better. "Ethan, did we have plans? I wouldn't be surprised if I'd missed them, because I can't find my—"

"Planner," Ethan interrupted, lifting the treasured book with one hand and opening the door a bit wider.

Claire rushed over and threw her arms around his neck. Squeezing tight, before releasing him from her death hold, she shouted, "Thank you, thank you, thank you. You saved me."

He shrugged and sent her a warm smile, his blue eyes taunting her. "Let me guess. You were in here freaking out because you didn't know every minute of every day for the next week."

She pouted. "Hey, I'm not that bad. I have a tight schedule with everything happing in the next few months. I don't know how I'm going to get it all done, but having this," she snatched the book from his grip and waved it in the air, "helps a ton. Seriously, thank you."

Granny sidled up behind Claire and whispered in her ear, "You don't need that thing. It's going to make you sick. Bad fruit. Remember what I said." Then, she turned to Ethan. "Young man, it's always a pleasure to see you. I'm guessing you two will want to take a stroll, hold hands, and be romantic, so I'll skedaddle." She walked past the couple but turned in the doorway before leaving, settling her gaze on Claire. "Bad. Fruit." Then, she walked down the hallway, probably on her way to tease and torment Albert about the lunch menu.

Ethan sent Claire a quizzical look. "What's with the obsession about fruit?"

Claire shook her head. "It's nothing. Granny's in one of her moods where she feels the need to impart ancient wisdom to me. She's done it ever since I was a kid. Granny always harped on me to wear a coat when I went outside so I wouldn't catch a cold. In medical school, I found out that wasn't true. She means well, but I don't place a ton of weight on her weird advice—like avoiding bad fruit."

He shrugged and accepted her answer. "Okay." Lifting his hand, he waved her over. "Come here. I want to tell you something."

She arched a brow and took a few steps closer to the man who had captured her heart and filled it with love.

"What do you want to tell me?" The corners of her lips tugged upward.

He leaned his head down next to her ear and whispered, "I love you, Dr. Claire Thomson, and I can't wait to marry you." He turned his face and pressed his lips against her cheek, letting them linger for a moment before pulling away. He sent her a smile and shoved his hands in the pockets of his pressed khaki shorts. The sapphire blue polo shirt he wore complimented his eyes.

She met his gaze, and her heart pounded harder. "I love you, too. I can't wait for the wedding either, but how do you feel about becoming a king?" Flicking her eyes down at the planner in her hands, the weight of the upcoming months weighed upon her.

Money and position didn't matter to Ethan. However, a nagging worry circled Claire's mind that he wouldn't want the royal life and all the expectations involved with it. She frowned.

Ethan stepped forward and placed a gentle hand under her chin. "I want you. I'm ready to do whatever it takes to be with you, even if it means wearing a crown. Besides, it will drive Richard crazy, so that's a perk." He chuckled and gave her a quick peck on the lips.

Claire shook her head. "You're terrible. You can't lord your title over your brother." She paused, considering all the manipulative and vengeful things Richard had done or said. "Well, maybe a little lording…but only a little." She laughed and opened her planner. "Okay, now that you've found my life again, I've got to figure out how I'm going to accomplish everything in the next few months."

Claire flipped the pages forward and stopped on today's date. "There's not much time—not much time at all." She tapped her foot, running through all the things to do and the calls to make. "Oh, and don't forget, somewhere wedged in the middle of the next few weeks will be Oxmund Hospital's charity luncheon. I promised them I'd help plan it and give a speech—you know how I feel about public speaking."

Ethan's lips curved upward, and he stifled a laugh. "Oh, I know. Don't think I've forgotten the polo match."

She gave him a playful shove on the arm. "Hey, don't tease me. I couldn't help it that I dropped the microphone in a horse's, well, you know. I was nervous. Super nervous. I'm not sure any amount of royal lessons from the queen mother can fix that problem."

He rubbed her arms with his hands and squeezed her. "You'll do great."

She sent him a half-grin. "I don't have as much faith as you do, but I'll do my best." She peered at her planner and flipped back to today's date. Tapping the page riddled with pen marks and words circled in highlighter, she reminded him, "See. Today—lunch with the queen mother. I knew there was something important I had to do today. She wants to review the next week's activities and preparations for the coronation. You should join us." She closed the book and clutched it to her chest like a child's favorite toy.

He raised his brow and rubbed his chin, which had a day's worth of stubble. "I don't know... I'm not dressed for lunch with your grandmother, and I didn't even shave today. Are you sure she won't mind?"

"I'm sure. Please. Feeding you lunch is the least I can do for my valiant knight who rescued my planner from the dungeon of lost items." She placed the back of her hand to her forehead and feigned a damsel in distress pose.

He laughed and shook her head. "You're more like Granny than you know. Okay, you've got yourself a date. Let's have lunch with the queen mother and talk about all things coronation."

She hooked her arm in his and followed him out of the bedroom. "Can you think of any better way to spend your day?"

He glanced down at her as they walked and grinned. "I cannot."

Neither could Claire.

He kissed the top of her head and led her down the stairs and toward the grand banquet room to plan their future.

For the first time today, hope filled Claire's chest. She could do it all. In a few months, she'd become queen of Amorley, Mrs. Ethan Kane, and the proud owner of her own happily ever after.

Chapter 2

Claire's royal grandmother, the queen mother, sat at the far end of the dining table. She dipped her head in a slight nod as the pair entered the room.

Ethan took his seat at the table across from Claire. He lifted the napkin in front of him and placed it in his lap before returning his gaze to find Claire's.

She beamed at him for several seconds before her smile faded. The blood drained from her complexion. Her lips parted, and she whispered, "No."

He frowned, wondering what had caused the look of concern to paint her face. Turning in his seat, he cast a glance over his shoulder and found the answer—Maurelle.

She wore a long, black dress that slithered behind her as she approached the table. Ethan snapped his head forward and reached a hand toward Claire. He placed his hand on top of hers and squeezed it.

"Well, what do we have here? A family reunion? My invitation must have gotten lost in the mail."

Claire cleared her throat and shifted in her seat. "Uh, I thought you were spending time at the summer castle. When did you arrive?"

Maurelle sank into an empty chair next to Ethan so she could face her stepdaughter. She crossed her hands in her lap and squared her shoulders before answering, "Yes, I did take a respite at the summer castle, but as you know plans change."

Ethan darted his eyes between Claire and her stepmother, wanting to protect his fiancé from the impending blow Maurelle would likely deliver. No way she had returned to Evercliff because she missed her family—not Maurelle's style.

Claire pressed her lips together in a thin line. "Sometimes plans change, I suppose. Fortunately, ours haven't. We're still excited about the upcoming coronation and then the wedding a few short weeks after it."

Maurelle sneered. "The coronation—I'm glad you brought it up because that's one reason I shortened my vacation and returned early."

Ethan's chest tightened. Here it was—the ammunition Maurelle had carried to drop on the two of them.

Instead of divulging the reason for her unexpected appearance, Maurelle picked up her napkin, placed it in her lap, and turned to the queen mother. "Ma'am, I hope it won't be any trouble if I stay for the next few weeks or perhaps longer."

The queen mother frowned. "Well, no, I see no reason why you cannot stay as long as your intentions are pure."

Maurelle's hand flew to her chest. "I'm hurt. Of course, my intentions for this family and the crown are pure. I've always wanted the best for Amorley and its people."

The queen mother nodded and retrieved her fork, digging into her chicken. "Good."

Claire followed her grandmother's lead and picked up a fork, taking a bite from her plate. She sat mid-chew when Maurelle released her bomb.

Maurelle swallowed a bite and smirked. She cocked her head to the side and stared at Claire. "I've discovered something of interest during my time away from Evercliff. I used my newfound free time to learn more about the country's history and its Constitution."

Uh oh.

She lowered her fork and leaned closer to Claire as if ready to share a secret. "Did you know that the coronation of the heir to the throne must take place within one year of the previous ruler's death? If I'm not mistaken, that would mean the coronation must happen within," she tapped out the days on her fingers, "a month."

Claire gagged on her chicken at this revelation. "A month," she croaked.

Dipping her brow in a look of faux-concern, Maurelle nodded. "I'm afraid so. It doesn't leave much time, does it? Of course, if you aren't prepared to step into the role, then the footnote I found also indicated the crown would pass to the next blood heir—my son. No one would blame you if you weren't ready for such responsibility in a month."

Claire opened her mouth to answer but closed it once again.

Ethan cleared his throat. "She'll be ready. We'll all help her, and there's an entire castle staff on hand to assist with plans. We'll have to move the timeline up, that's all."

Claire glanced toward the queen mother and raised her brow.

The queen mother tilted her head and clasped her hands together in front of her on the table. "I've never heard of such a rule, Maurelle. Are you sure it's in the Constitution?"

Maurelle whipped her head toward the queen mother, and a triumphant smile spread across her face. "I'm sure, but as I said if you cannot prepare Claire by then—"

Raising a hand, the queen mother interrupted Maurelle, "Nonsense. Claire's an intelligent woman, and my staff and I can ready her in time. You'll forgive me, however, if I have the castle's attorney investigate this clause."

Maurelle leaned back in her chair. "Of course. I assure you the footnote exists and is legal." Pausing for a moment, she drew in a breath. "I almost forgot to mention—the Constitution also states you must be engaged."

Claire scrunched her brow. "I don't see how that's a problem. I am engaged. We're planning a wedding."

Maurelle's lips pressed together and drew up slightly at the ends. "Oh, you know how sometimes unexpected obstacles occur, and things don't work out as planned. Something to consider." She peered at the watch on her left wrist and raised her head, meeting the queen mother's eyes once more. "If you will excuse me, I think I'll take a short nap. The trip here exhausted me, and I need my beauty rest."

Ethan gasped. No one left the dinner table before the queen mother.

The color had left the queen mother's face now, too. "Very well."

Standing, Maurelle tossed a plastic smile in Claire's direction. "Good to see you again. Enjoy your lunch." Then, she spun around and strolled out of the room.

Exhaling, Ethan released Claire's hand. "Well, she brought rainbows and sunbeams with her, didn't she?"

Lifting a hand to her head, Claire's fingers trembled as she tucked a piece of her sunshine-colored locks behind her ear. "Yeah. Like having lunch with a winter storm."

"More like a tsunami." Ethan chuckled.

Claire rewarded him with her first grin in the past thirty minutes.

The queen mother broke the tension. "Everything will be fine. Please don't worry about Maurelle. Even if what she says is true and we have to move the coronation date up, we can do it. It will be a tight timeline, and there's certainly a mountain of things to cover in four weeks, but we'll find a way. You're not alone."

Dropping her hand back on the table, Claire whispered, "Okay."

Only the quiver that remained in Claire's hand betrayed her. He prayed everything would be okay, but knowing Maurelle, he had his doubts. He didn't dare share this opinion with Claire, though. "Yeah, don't worry about any of it. It will be okay." He hoped.

Chapter 3

Claire awoke the following morning drenched in sweat. The remnants of her dream trailed at the edges of her mind. She'd been running through a dark forest trying to find her mother so she could ask for advice about the future. The longer she ran, the heavier her legs grew, and Claire never gained any ground—as if she were on a treadmill to nowhere.

Pushing her matted, damp hair off her forehead, Claire sat up in bed. A psychotherapist wouldn't have to delve far into that dream to find the deeper meaning— she didn't know what to do. Should she give up and not take the Crown after all?

She and Ethan could head off into the sunset together and live a simple, nonroyal life. Would she make a good queen? Sometimes Claire still had her doubts. She'd hoped to hide behind her grandmother's royal apron for three to six months longer and ease herself into her newfound responsibilities. Plus, she had only recently begun her efforts with Oxmund Hospital's charity.

Leaning forward, Claire dropped her head into her hands. *God, what do I do?* When she raised her head again, her eyes fell on her Bible on the nightstand.

Reaching for it, she plopped it on her lap and flipped through it aimlessly. Running her fingers down the page, she paused in the middle and stared at the words before her.

"Be strong and courageous. Do not be afraid; do not be discouraged, for the Lord your God will be with you wherever you go." Josh. 1:9.

Huh. Don't be afraid. Easier said than done. However, the last part tugged at Claire's heart. Would God be with her on this journey? Did she not have to go it alone? As she pondered this thought, her door creaked open, and Wilson bounded into the room. He dove for the bed unsuccessfully. After his third attempt, Claire took pity on him and reached down, scooping him up with two hands. "Oof. You're huge. Pretty soon, I won't be able to lift you."

Wilson grinned and let his tongue hang out the side of his mouth. He panted after all his effort, sneezed once, and then heaved himself on the comforter with an exhausted sigh.

My thoughts exactly. Claire stretched her arms overhead and followed Wilson's example, resting her head on the pillow. Still, her eyes darted toward the planner on her desk, beckoning her from across the room. She might not be alone, but if Claire didn't get some work done today, then she'd not be any closer to becoming a wife or a queen.

She swung her legs over the side of the bed and shoved her feet into fluffy slippers. Shuffling across the room, Claire made her way toward the wooden desk. The aroma of bacon and eggs wafted from downstairs, begging her to tackle breakfast before one of her many tasks. Still, her eyes flitted toward the planner once more. Breakfast would have to wait.

Claire pulled the chair back and sank into it. She found herself still reeling from the events of the previous day. Her dream (or more of a nightmare) didn't help things, either. Sitting at the desk, she stared at her planner and let the black ink of the items on her to-do list swirl before her eyes. They created a dizzying dark blob, and her chest tightened.

One month? She only had one month to sort out her life. One month to learn how to become a queen. One month to conquer the coronation, wedding, and hospital plans. Calm, deep breaths. I can do it. Right? Maybe. Okay, maybe not.

Suddenly the air in the bedroom suffocated her. She dashed to the window and yanked it upward, releasing a fresh, warm breeze into the room. The sheer white curtains swayed, looking much more relaxed and carefree than Claire.

Her heart rate had almost returned to normal when the bedroom door burst open. "I just heard. I can't believe it. Well, that's not true. I can believe it, but it still stinks." Claire's granny stood in the doorway wearing a polyester orange tracksuit and matching lipstick. She crossed her arms in front of her chest and tapped her foot. "Well, what are you going to do?"

Claire walked around the end of the bed and joined her granny. She wrapped her arms around Granny. "I guess you found out Maurelle's returned for a repeat performance."

Granny made a clucking sound with her tongue. "I don't like it—not one bit. That woman cannot have good intentions returning to Evercliff. She's set her sights on the Crown."

Claire started to speak, but Granny lifted a hand. "No, I know what you're going to say. We can't assume the worst about people. Maybe she's changed. Perhaps she's ready to put the past behind her. All that stuff I taught you growing up in church—and it's true. But—"

Claire interrupted her Granny's ethical monologue, "But nothing. This time is no different than the last. She wants to rule. Maurelle took jabs at my relationship with Ethan and mentioned that the Crown will pass to Eric if my coronation doesn't take place within a month." She jutted out her lower lip and blew out a breath, causing the loose tendrils around her face to move out of her eyes. "Your concern is valid. She's up to no good."

Granny punched the air. "I knew it. I knew it. Ooh, that woman. Don't you worry—I've got your back. Isn't that what kids say today?"

Frowning, Claire stepped closer to Granny.

Granny fiddled with one of her earrings and tilted her head. "What's wrong?"

"I don't know if I'll be able to finish all this stuff in a month. It panicked me to think about tackling the wedding, the coronation, the hospital duties, the charity, and everything else within a few months. Now that I have to condense all that work into thirty days—I don't know if I can do it."

Shaking her head, Granny lifted Claire's chin with her arthritic finger and forced Claire to meet her eyes. "You can do it, but you can't do it all alone. You need help."

Claire marveled at the truth in her granny's words. She smiled and hugged her granny again. Inhaling the familiar scent of lilacs from her granny's perfume instantly eased her anxiety.

Granny laughed out loud.

Claire leaned back and looked into her granny's eyes. Raising a brow, she asked, "What's so funny?"

Still snickering, Granny tried to collect herself. "I just thought of something."

"What?" Claire asked.

"Old Queenie hasn't seen the new puppy, has she?" Granny's blue eyes twinkled with mischief.

Claire frowned again. "No, why?"

"Woohoo. I didn't think so. Oh boy, I can't wait to see the look on Maurelle's face when she finds out there's another canine in the castle."

Claire's throat tightened again, and she swallowed hard over the lump forming in her throat. "What about what happened to Milo?" she whispered.

Granny's face darkened. "I won't let anything happen to Sir Wilson. She won't lay a finger on him—not a finger. If I have to follow her around like a tracking beam, I'll do it. Okay?"

Claire pulled in a breath. She couldn't imagine anything happening to Wilson, the puppy Ethan had given her shortly after Milo's untimely death. She didn't think Milo's fate had been an accident, and though Claire couldn't prove it, she suspected her stepmother's involvement. "Okay."

Granny nodded and reached for Claire's hand. "Good. Now, how about you and I take a short walk around the garden with Wilson to clear our heads. Then, we can find Albert and start on your to-do list."

Claire smiled and took her granny's hand, thankful to still have this wonderful woman in her life. Since losing her mom over a year ago, Claire had come to rely on Granny more and more for motherly advice. "Sounds like a plan. Thanks, Granny."

"No problem, sweet girl. I love you."

Then, the two Thomson women left Claire's bedroom ready to take on the world—or at least the first few items on Claire's insurmountable task list.

Chapter 4

Granny interlocked her arm with Claire's and led the way out of Evercliff's rear entrance.

The sun broke through the early morning clouds, providing a bright ray of warmth on Claire's face.

Granny turned her head toward Claire and smiled. "What's the first thing to tackle on the list?"

Claire dipped her head, and her eyes skimmed over the never-ending list of to-do items. "Well, the wedding must take a backseat to the coronation--at least for now. I guess if we could get a guest list together for Coronation Day, write my speech, and decide on a dress for the event, that would be a start."

Patting Claire's hand, she tilted her head. "Easy peasy. Piece of cake and all that other euphemistic nonsense. The point is—we can do it."

A wave of relief washed over Claire, and her shoulders relaxed. "Thanks for helping me. I don't know what I'd do without you."

Granny winked. "You got it—anything for family. Let's start with the fun part—the dress. Were you thinking—"

The queen mother appeared behind Claire and her granny, interrupting their walk, "There you are. I've been looking for you everywhere. We have lots to discuss in preparation for your Coronation Day,"

Claire sent her grandmother a grin and nodded toward her list. "That's what we were doing. Granny offered to help me with the plans." Claire imagined everyone at the coronation wearing tracksuits and piles of costume jewelry. Granny would love that. She supposed the idea of Granny contributing to the Coronation Day plans sent shock waves through the queen mother. She chuckled, considering this thought.

The queen mother pulled her brow downward. "What's so funny?"

Claire tossed off the idea as both possible and unthinkable. "I'm sorry—it's nothing." She cast a furtive glance toward Granny and swore she saw an understanding, teasing glint in her eye. Sometimes that woman could read her mind.

The queen mother took a spot next to Claire's other side and fell into step with the pair. "Very well. Now then, we have much to do in a month. I'd hoped to have longer, but there you have it. What's that phrase all the young people toss around? It is what it is. Well put, I'd say."

"Me, too. We thought we could start with deciding on my gown for the coronation. Did you have something specific in mind?" Claire raised a brow as she found her grandmother's gaze.

The queen mother's eyes lit up, and she quickened her pace. "I did. I had hoped you might wear the dress I wore to your grandfather's coronation. It's tradition for the successor to wear a garment from a past ruler's ensemble. I doubt you'd want to wear your father's coat, so I thought you could borrow something of mine. We could attach your father's coat of arms pin to it."

Claire's mouth went dry, and the blood left her face. It's not that she was a fashionista or superficial. Still, she'd hoped to select a modern gown, and she certainly hadn't envisioned attaching a large pin to her dress. Not wanting to hurt the queen mother's feelings, Claire swallowed hard and pasted a forced smile on her face instead of sharing these sentiments. "That's sounds lovely." It did not. However, her mom always said to put other's feelings before one's own.

The queen mother clapped her hands together. "Wonderful. You'll love it. I'll have Albert dig it out of the royal vestibule so it can air out before you try it on. Why don't we reconvene after dinner and see how it fits?"

Claire screwed her face in confusion. "Royal vestibule?"

Smiling, the queen mother nodded. "It's a fancy closet. We keep all the important articles, jewels, and clothing there. The contents of it are worth a small fortune."

Wow. "Great. That sounds great." It did not, but Claire couldn't say no to tradition. Plus, based on the excitement on her grandmother's face, Claire would break her heart if she turned down the offer.

The queen mother peered at the wristwatch on her left arm. "I hate to part from the walk—the gardens are so beautiful this time of year—but I need to find Albert and get your dress ready. I've got several other items to attend to in preparation for the coronation. The guest list currently stands at ten thousand and I've got to shave off at least two thousand people. It's difficult to know who to edit as I don't want to offend anyone."

Eight thousand people? Claire's throat tightened. "Um, Grandmother, I assume I'll be giving my acceptance speech to all of them?" The only thing that sounded more daunting than wearing a thousand-year-old musty dress was wearing a thousand-year-old musty dress in front of a circus of people.

The queen mother grinned. "Of course. Well, I must be off—enjoy the rest of your walk. I'll see you both later." Then, Claire's grandmother strode to the castle, oblivious to the small bombs she'd dropped on her granddaughter.

"You look that same shade of green you turned the night we tried sushi from that new food truck. Remember that night?" Granny shook her head. "What a doozy."

Claire patted her face. It did feel clammy. "I'm fine," she whispered, unconvinced.

Granny arched a draw-on brow. "You're sure?"

Claire's lips pulled into a thin smile. "No, but what choice do I have?"

Granny shrugged. "You always have a choice. We could still hop a plane and skedaddle to Boston—take Ethan with us. Start over. However, I know you'll make a great queen and can help the Amorley people."

The edges of Claire's lips tugged upward a bit more. "I hope you're right." Claire sent a silent prayer for wisdom to God and continued down the pebbled path, focusing on her steps as the worries of the day circled her mind.

Chapter 5

The rain lessened as Ethan drove through town. He parked the car and the drizzle turned to a sprinkle and stopped as suddenly as it had begun. Shaking the raindrops off his hair, he shoved his hands in his pants pockets as he slowly took each step to the entrance of Michael's townhouse. He raised his hand and rapped on the door three times. Staring at his gleaming dress shoes, he waited.

A bleary-eyed Michael, Ethan's best friend, answered the door. "What's up? I didn't know you were coming by." He rubbed his face with the palm of his hand and yawned. Squinting his eyes, he tilted his head and peered at the sun peeking through the ever-overcast sky. "What time is it?"

Ethan ran a hand through his hair and shifted his weight. "It's," he glanced at his watch and lifted his eyes to meet Michael's, "seven-thirty a.m. I'm sorry. I should have called—I didn't think." After getting up before sunrise this morning, Ethan had decided to his office early.

Somehow, he'd veered off course in the direction of his friend's road on the way to work. Ethan had reviewed all the events of the past few days several times. Even though he wanted to marry Claire, the rest of the mess left him unsure about the likelihood of it happening. Michael would know what to do—he always did. "I can go. I didn't mean to wake you." The early morning breeze blew, carrying with it an earthly scent typical for Amorley after a fresh rainfall. He turned to leave.

Michael waved his friend to come inside. "It's fine. Don't worry about it. I need to start work anyways. I should thank you. I've got a meeting at ten, and I should head in beforehand to prepare for it. I stayed up until two a.m. working on logistics for the coronation. Parliament and the queen mother have different viewpoints on some of these issues, as you can imagine."

Ethan sent his friend a smile. Michael's law degree and role in Parliament kept him busy.

Opening the door wider, Michael turned and retreated into his home, still wearing his bathrobe.

Following his friend inside, Ethan sank into one of the two chairs he'd shared with Michael the last time he'd visited. He recalled their conversation about how to help Claire take the throne while maintaining her medical pursuits. Ethan smiled at how his friend had helped them succeed. Indeed, he'd provide some wisdom now.

Michael took his place across from Ethan, swiped his hands down his face and leaned back. He rested his head against the chair, closing his eyes. "Okay, so what's got you so worried? I know you're a morning person and a hard worker, but if you're at my house by seven-thirty, that means you've been up for two hours already."

Ethan sighed. "It's complicated."

"If we're going to have a serious discussion at this horrendous hour, I've got to have some coffee. You want any?" Michael placed his hands on his knees and heaved himself out of the chair, stumbling to the kitchen.

Ethan sent his friend a smile. "That'd be great. Thanks again, mate."

Ten minutes later, the two friends sat across from one another again, steaming mugs of black coffee in their hands. The aroma of the dark roast revived Michael and sharpened Ethan's mind.

Michael placed his mug on a small table next to his chair and leaned forward, clasping his hands together and resting his elbows on his thighs. "What's the problem this time?"

"Well, remember how the queen mother had planned the coronation to take place several months from now?" Ethan took a quick draw of hot liquid from his cup.

Michael arched a brow. "Yeah."

"Remember how we were going to do the wedding after that—take our time so Claire could settle into her role as both a queen and physician?"

Shrugging, Michael answered, "Yes, so what happened."

"Everything is a mess, and I don't know what to do about any of it."

"You and Claire looked like the picture of happiness and romance—like some cover for a happily ever after brochure. What changed?"

Ethan took another sip but found it hard to swallow. He choked down the coffee and placed his mug on the table with Michael's. Pressing his lips into a firm line, he caught Michael's gaze. "Everything. Maurelle came back."

Michael's eyes widened. "No. Not possible. I thought she left--banished to the ends of the earth or something."

"Or something—and it is possible. Maurelle spent 'vacation time' at the summer castle. I assumed—no hoped—she'd stay there indefinitely. However, she made an appearance yesterday and told Claire that there's a footnote in the Constitution stating that if Claire isn't engaged and crowned queen in a month, then the crown will pass to her step-brother, Eric."

"Wow. Okay. I see why you're driving around Amorley at the break of dawn. Still, it should be doable, right? You two are engaged. You're happy."

"For now," Ethan sighed.

Michael frowned. "What's that supposed to mean. You are happy, aren't you? Why wouldn't you be engaged in a month? Don't you love Claire?"

Tears stung Ethan's eyes, but he refused to cry in front of his friend. "Of course, I love her. I'd do anything for her. I'm worried that Maurelle will create problems. What if Claire changes her mind about staying in Amorley? What if she changes her mind about me? Not to mention the problems with my family—my father hates me, my mother's avoiding my calls, and Richard is, well, Richard."

"You're ridiculous. That girl loves you, and how difficult can it be to sidestep anything Maurelle throws your way?"

"I guess you're right, but what about the coronation? Claire's nervous about it. The queen mother had planned to give Claire more royal lessons before passing the Crown to her. Do you think the two of us will be ready to lead Amorley in less than thirty days?"

Michael jumped from his seat. "Follow me. I want to show you something."

Ethan jerked in surprise at the unexpected movement, nearly knocking his coffee cup and its contents off the table beside him. He started to fuss at his friend, but the seriousness in Michael's eyes caused Ethan to oblige him. He rose from his seat and followed Michael down the hallway toward his office.

Michael went inside and made quite the picture taking his seat in the leather chair still wearing his robe. He looked like a hospital escapee. Rifling through a stack of papers crisscrossed on the top of the desk, Michael muttered, "I know it's here somewhere."

"What?" Ethan asked.

"Aha. Found it. I knew I'd seen it the other day. I decided to get my office in order, and while going through old paperwork, I found this." He lifted his hand, which held a slightly wrinkled photograph.

Ethan leaned closer and squinted his eyes. He stared at a picture of him and Michael from their university days. Ethan, Michael, Ethan's father, his mother, and even his brother, Richard, sat around a dinner table at a fancy restaurant gazing at the camera. All of them wore smiles, unaware of the massive fallout yet to come. "We looked happy."

Ethan remembered the day well--parent's weekend. Ethan's father had been softer back then if only a little. His expectations still ran high, but he hadn't gone into full-on world domination mode yet. Younger by a few years, Richard still looked up to his big brother back then. Oh, sure, they'd had their share of friendly and not-so-friendly competition even then, but it hadn't gone to the current extremes. A knot formed in Ethan's throat, and he struggled to swallow it away.

Michael must have seen the pain cross Ethan's face because his smile fell. "Hey, I didn't mean to upset you, but I wanted to show you this guy." He pointed to the younger, more carefree version of Ethan in the photograph. The young man wore a relaxed grin, sun-kissed blond hair from time spent on a boat the day prior, and he even had his arm draped across his brother's chair.

Ethan shrugged. "Yeah, that guy looks happy—like he doesn't have a single care."

"He does, but that's not why I showed it to you."

Ethan raised his forehead. "Why did you show it to me, then?"

Tapping at the photograph for emphasis, Michael stared hard at Ethan. "I wanted to remind you that this guy is still somewhere inside you—the guy who didn't back down from challenges. He never said no to my crazy plans, even if they landed us stuck in the middle of the sea on a boat without gasoline. His family loved him—and still does even though they aren't acting like it right now. Even if your brother's gone a little crazy."

Ethan looked away, the picture of the happy family piercing his heart. "I don't know about that. My father doesn't share your opinion. The last discussion I had with him resulted in him telling me I'm out of the family, and Richard had replaced me."

Michael sat a firm hand on Ethan's shoulder.

Ethan turned and glanced at his longtime friend.

"I don't believe it. That's what he said, but he didn't mean it. And Richard, well, I don't know about Richard.

He's always looked up to you and probably dealt with a lot of jealousy, but I bet he still cares in his way."

Ethan chuckled at this summarization. "Yes, but what can I do about it? They won't speak to me."

"You can pray about it. Trust God to work out things and lean on Him. You don't have to do it all yourself. Neither does Claire. You both have lots of people ready to help out and ensure the coronation is a success. Plus, your father will come around—eventually."

Ethan raised a brow. "You think so?"

Michael smiled. "I do. Now, come on." He pointed to a younger Ethan in the photo. "Let's get you back to this guy. How about we take a ride before you tackle anything else today? It will do you good—clear your head."

Ethan nodded. "Maybe you're right. A ride sounds good."

"Absolutely. Fresh air is what you need. Let's go." Michael hopped up from his chair, already making his way to the office door.

Ethan put out a hand and stopped Michael.

Michael froze and frowned. "What's wrong now?"

"Oh, nothing." Ethan smirked. "I wondered if you planned to go horseback riding in your robe."

Michael looked down at his attire and gave Ethan and teasing punch. "Haha. Thanks. No. I'll change. Hang on." Michael headed toward his bedroom at the end of the hallway.

Ethan followed down the hallway and called after him through the closed bedroom door, "You could start a new look—casual loungewear jodhpurs."

Michael's door opened a crack, and he chucked a pillow at Ethan's head before slamming it again. "Funny.

You're funny," he answered in a muffled voice from the other side of the door.

Ethan glanced at the picture of his past self in his hand, smiling with his family and friends. "I am, aren't, I?" Maybe Michael was right, and he needed to trust God and let go. Everything would work out with Claire, the coronation, and his family—right?

Chapter 6

Claire glided past a large mirror in the hallway on the way to meet the queen mother, Granny, and Ethan for dinner. She'd spent most of the day with Granny and Albert discussing the to-do list for the coronation and checking items off the list. They were the smaller items, but, still—it counted.

Buoyed with confidence from seeing some things accomplished, Claire smiled at her reflection and held her head higher. She could do this. Pulling her shoulders back, she stood tall—the way the queen mother had taught her during their first royal lesson together. This confidence lasted until Claire arrived at the banquet room's entrance. Her eyes fell upon two dinner guests— Maurelle and her son and Claire's half-brother, Eric.

Everyone at the table rose as Claire entered except Maurelle and the queen mother. Not seeing the queen mother stand was expected—tradition didn't dictate it until Claire took the throne as the queen herself. However, Maurelle was making a point in her defiance.

"There you are—we wondered what could be keeping you. Of course, with your plate full of responsibilities and so little time to prepare for your coronation, I understand why you're late to dinner." Maurelle placed a forced smile on her face.

Eric sat to the right side of his mother in the middle of the table. At one end resided the queen mother and to her right sat Granny and then Ethan.

Claire's half-brother raised his head when Maurelle spoke, and his gaze laser-beamed toward the recipient of his mother's barbs. He offered Claire an apologetic smile.

Claire cleared her throat and said a silent prayer for patience before responding to her stepmother's attack, "Good evening. I apologize for my tardiness, but as you mentioned, I've had a lot to do today. You'll be pleased to know coronation plans are moving along smoothly." Claire might have embellished how much she'd accomplished, but she wouldn't tell Maurelle that.

Maurelle sneered and muttered, "Wonderful." Then, she lifted the napkin off her plate and placed it in her lap as if dismissing the subject.

Claire turned her attention to Eric. Her half-brother didn't seem like an unpleasant person, but his vengeful mother had handicapped their relationship. Still, Claire's mother's voice resonated in her mind to be kind always. "Eric, I'm Claire. I've heard a lot about you." She closed the distance between them and extended her hand. "Nice to meet you."

Eric raised his head and locked his green eyes on Claire. A genuine smile replaced his apologetic one, and he shook her hand. "Nice to meet you, too. You aren't late—we just sat down."

Claire's shoulders relaxed, and gratitude washed over her. Eric didn't automatically hate her because she stood first in line for the Crown. "Thanks. Please, don't let me hold up things any longer." She hurried to the other side of the table and waited as Ethan rose and pulled out her chair. Sinking into it, she gazed up at him and sent him a warm smile.

He flashed her a quick wink before taking his place at the table again.

"Now then, if we are all ready." The queen mother plucked a small gold bell from the table and gave it a ring.

Albert materialized at her side wearing his usual uniform of black pressed slacks and a suit jacket. Beads of sweat puddled across his forehead, and his face flushed. Bowing at the waist, he asked, "Ma'am, how may I be of service."

The queen mother placed the bell on the table and turned her head toward Albert. "We are ready to begin the meal now."

Albert gave another slight bow. "Yes, of course, Ma'am. I'll let the kitchen staff know and begin the meal promptly." He turned and rushed toward the kitchen.

Huh. That was different. Albert was always serious—formal—but not like that.

Granny leaned around the back of Ethan's chair and whispered in Claire's ear, "What was that? Old Albie looked like he'd come from a funeral." She gestured with her thumb toward the kitchen.

"I don't know, but you're right. Something—"

Albert reappeared and bolted to Claire's side. He bowed at her and then lowered his head and voice, so no one else at the table could hear, "Ma'am, if you could join me in the kitchen for a moment. There's, uh, a situation I need you to address."

Claire frowned and wondered what could have happened in the time since she'd left him during their planning session earlier. It wasn't like Albert to act secretive. She nodded and rose from her seat and flicked her eyes toward the queen mother. "Grandmother, would you excuse me for a minute?"

The queen mother raised an eyebrow. "Very well, but please hurry. Dinner's going to be late as it is."

Claire nodded and stood, following Albert to the kitchen.

As Albert closed the door behind them, he wrung his hands.

Claire raised a brow. "Albert, what's wrong?"

He paced back and forth across the kitchen floor. "It's Wilson. He ate the main course for dinner—the turkey. Also, he's covered in mud. When he stole the turkey from the kitchen table, he took off with it and buried it in the flowerbeds."

Wilson barked.

Claire glanced in the kitchen corner where her rascal dog sat. Now mud-coated, he held his prize between his teeth. Only a leg had survived and hung from his mouth. He looked like he would play a game of tug of war with Claire if she tried to take it from him.

Claire gasped and her hand flew to her mouth. "What do we do?" She gestured toward the turkey leg caked in mud and her puppy. She couldn't help but picture the look on Maurelle's face when she found out what another one of Claire's canine friends had done. Her heartrate increased, and her palms began to sweat. What if Maurelle tried to do something to Wilson? Claire wouldn't put it past her—not after what happened to Milo. Sure, she couldn't prove Maurelle had poisoned her longtime friend and buddy, but Claire suspected her the culprit.

"I don't know, Ma'am. Even though the queen mother is understanding, she won't be thrilled with this news. This is the third time this week he's stolen food from the kitchen and about the hundredth hole he's dug in the garden. I'm afraid this hole caused a casualty of the queen mother's roses. She loves those flowers."

Albert turned around and called the cook, "Emily, what do we have on hand to serve tonight? Besides, the deconstructed turkey."

Emily grabbed the hand towel draped across her shoulder and wiped the sweat from her forehead that the hot summer day and the muggy kitchen had caused. She walked to the refrigerator and opened the silver door. Bending at the waist, she peered inside. "Let's see. We have some cold cuts to make sandwiches later this week and some leftover onion gravy. Ooh, I still have some Amorley pudding. I could add the gravy as an appetizer and serve a cold meat and cheese platter with some vegetables for the main course. It's not fancy, but it works."

Albert nodded. "Thanks. You're right—not fancy, but it will have to do." He turned to face Claire. "Go back in there and stall the meal."

Claire raised an eyebrow. A trickle of sweat trailed its way down her back. "How do you want me to do that?"

Tell them about the hospital charity and how things are going at work. The queen mother finds your medical stories fascinating."

Claire fanned herself. "Super. More time to spend with Maurelle."

Albert dipped his head. "Try not to let her get to you, ma'am. Remember, you're the one becoming the queen. She can't stand in the way of your destiny."

Accepting the truth in Albert's advice, Claire nodded and walked to the door. She placed her hand on the door and paused. Peering over her shoulder, she caught Albert's eye. "Thanks."

He smiled then his mouth settled into a serious line again. "Stall."

She grinned. "Will do." At least she'd try. She shoved open the door and marched into the dining room with all the confidence she could muster. Claire recalled her royal lessons with her grandmother—shoulders back, head tall, eyes forward. Nice, even strides. Claire walked to the table, and again, Ethan pulled her chair out for her. "Thank you," she whispered to him.

Ethan leaned in and lowered his voice so only Claire could hear, "Everything okay?"

Claire murmured in return, "Wilson."

He sent her a half-smile and took his seat.

"My dear, is something wrong?" The queen mother peered at Claire over the top of her glasses and waited for a response.

With a toss of her hand, Claire waved away her grandmother's concern. "No, not at all. Albert wanted to inform me about something we'd discussed earlier regarding the coronation. Which reminds me, do you mind if I invite the administrators from the hospital to the coronation? As an act of goodwill?"

Her grandmother frowned at the shift in the conversation. Still, she didn't press for more information. "Yes, that's fine. Leave their names with

Albert and my private secretary can add them to the guest list. How is your charitable work going?"

Claire's posture relaxed. She loved discussing the hospital charity. Patients held a special place in her heart. After the coronation and her wedding, Claire could finally focus on her marriage and medical work. Of course, she'd have Amorley matters as well, but she hoped things might slow down a bit once all the pomp and circumstance of the coronation passed. "It's great. I'm only seeing a few patients a week right now and attending tons of meetings for the charity. Hopefully, in a few months I can increase my caseload." Claire lifted her water glass to her lips and took a sip.

"Good. Don't forget to allow time to start a family. It's something you and Ethan will have to talk about soon. We'll need an heir to the throne."

Claire choked on her water. She slammed her cup down and sputtered, gasping for air. "Grandmother!" she croaked. Her eyes darted toward Ethan to assess what level of freaked-out he'd achieved, but his face remained surprisingly calm.

Ethan caught her gaze, and a small smile tugged at the corners of his mouth. "It's fine. Believe me, if my parents were still speaking to me, they'd be discussing the same thing. My mother couldn't wait to become a grandmother." He looked at the queen mother, and a wistful expression glazed over his eyes.

Claire prayed every night for reconciliation between Ethan and his parents—that somehow his father would awaken one day and realize how ridiculous he'd behaved. She shook her head—she couldn't do anything about it right now except support her fiancé and pray for God's intervention.

Albert entered the room, followed by a parade of servers. They placed a plate of cold cuts and cheeses along with a dish of Amorley pudding in front of each guest.

The queen mother flicked her eyes toward Albert and sent him a quizzical look. "I thought we were to have turkey today. I went over all the meals in the menu book earlier this week, and I specifically recall turkey for today." She tipped her nose downward, peering over the top of her glasses at Albert.

A flush of red filled Albert's cheeks, and he bowed at the waist. He glanced at Claire briefly before meeting the queen mother's gaze again. "Yes, Ma'am, you are correct. However, I thought with the heat of the day that the cold cuts might be nice. Also, you adore Amorley pudding, so I requested the cook make it for you. Is it acceptable?" He raised a brow.

She waved her hand and placed her napkin in her lap, folded in half. "No, that's fine. I'm glad I'm not losing my mind. Thank you, Albert." The queen mother lifted her fork with her left hand, indicating the meal could begin.

The rest of her guests followed suit and removed their napkins from the table before diving into the meal.

Albert straightened himself and cast a relieved look to Claire. He sent her a quick wink and then returned to the kitchen.

Claire exhaled. Albert hadn't snitched on Wilson. Not that her grandmother would be angry, but Claire didn't want to let her down, and she certainly didn't want to provide Maurelle with any further ammunition.

The rest of the meal passed uneventfully aside from a few snide remarks and verbal jabs from Maurelle. Eric, to his credit, remained pleasant. Claire asked him about his studies and interests. Despite her best efforts, she found herself unable to dislike her half-brother.

The conversation had hummed throughout the meal, punctuated with Granny's laughter. Now, it came to a lull, and everyone fell silent.

Claire lined her utensils up vertically on the center of her plate like her grandmother had taught her, indicating she'd finished eating.

The queen mother took her last bite and placed her utensils in the same position. Immediately, a swarm of waiters stepped forward from the walls where they'd stood. They gathered up the dishes and whisked them away.

The queen mother rose from her seat, and everyone else did the same. Her grandmother started to exit the dining room but paused at her granddaughter's seat. "Dear, don't forget we planned to practice for the coronation tomorrow. Eight a.m. Sharp. We'll meet in the study."

Claire resisted the urge to smack her forehead. She'd forgotten about coronation practice. Not knowing what it entailed, Claire suspected it would resemble royal lessons—no fun. Plus, she had a hospital charity event the day after tomorrow, and she'd promised to meet her boss and the event committee tomorrow afternoon to finalize plans. Oh, and she had to give a speech at the event. No pressure. Nothing on her plate. Deep breaths. She pasted a smile on her face. "Of course. See you then."

The queen mother nodded and left the room. Everyone else filed in line behind her.

She could handle it—right?

Chapter 7

Claire followed Albert to the study to meet her grandmother for their first coronation lesson. Sigh. She did not want to do this. Royal lessons proved hard enough—she could only imagine what today's instruction entailed.

As the pair crossed the entryway to the study, Albert cleared his throat before announcing her, "Your majesty, may I present Her Royal Highness."

The queen mother sat in her usual chair with her hands crossed in her lap. She wore a typical ensemble of a button-up jacket and skirt, nylons, and modest heels. Her short haircut and wire-rim glasses gave her a wise and regal appearance. "Come in. We have much to do today."

Claire took a few steps forward, and her eyes fell upon another figure in the room. Figure might not be the correct word—this woman demanded attention. Standing shy of five feet tall, her height did not subtract from her commanding presence. She'd dressed in all black from head to toe, wearing a long sleeve button-up shirt, firmly pressed pants, and sky-high heels. She had her hair in a bun so tight and smooth that Claire could almost see her reflection in it.

The woman's glasses made the pièce de résistance—she had on oversized, round sunglasses that were double the size of her face. Claire didn't know much about fashion, but they looked ridiculous. The woman must have taken a note from Maurelle's playbook because her lips bore the same ruby-red shade.

The stranger stepped forward and offered her hand to Claire. "Your Royal Highness, a pleasure to make your acquaintance. I am Mademoiselle Couture, and I will be assisting with your coronation and wedding attire when the time comes." She did a stiff, small curtsy and then resumed her robotic stance.

Was this woman for real? Did she know her last name meant tailor? Was it a name she gave herself, or did her parents bestow it upon her, paving the way for her destiny? So many questions.

The queen mother frowned and did the peering-over-her glasses thing. "My dear, don't stand there. Have you lost your manners and everything I taught you during our royal lessons? Please, take a seat so we can begin."

Claire shook her head. "I'm sorry, Grandmother. I didn't know we'd have company today." She took Mademoiselle Couture's hand and gave it a slight shake. "Nice to meet you." Darting her eyes toward the queen mother, Claire waited. Was she supposed to shake hands with this lady? The rules still perplexed her at times.

Her grandmother sent her a small smile and tilted her head toward the empty seat next to her.

Claire hurried over to the chair and sank into it, thankful she hadn't worn a bandage-like skirt for this round of lessons.

The queen mother dipped her head and then glanced toward the fashion guru. "Now, then. Let's get started, shall we?"

The sun-glassed woman sprang into action and clapped her hands together. An army of stylists, all dressed in black, entered the room on command.

The sudden noise startled Claire, and she jumped.

Her grandmother tilted her head and asked, "Did you have too much coffee this morning?"

Claire pulled in a deep breath and lowered her voice, "No more than usual. I'm a little nervous about coronation lessons, and Mrs. Couture makes for an intimidating figure. Remember, scrubs were my go-to attire before coming to the castle. Does she know I don't do super fancy?"

Pressing her lips together, the queen mother leaned a little closer. "Now you do. You're going to become queen, after all. Fancy is part of the job."

Trying not to scrunch her nose in displeasure, Claire straightened her posture and stared straight ahead, girding herself for whatever couture disasters awaited. Here we go.

Mademoiselle Couture walked toward Claire and placed her hands on her hips—not in a casual manner—more like a military commander preparing to give orders and enter battle.

Uh oh.

Mademoiselle Couture, still wearing her sunglasses, pressed her lips together before speaking, "Your Royal Highness, if I may, I need you to stand."

Claire obeyed and rose from her seat with trepidation. She smoothed out her knee-length blue skirt and stood tall the way her grandmother had taught her.

The woman finally removed her sunglasses with one hand and placed the tip of one of the earpieces in her mouth. She narrowed her eyes and surveyed the fashion canvas before her.

Claire could feel the woman's eyes scanning her from top to bottom. She shifted he weight, uncomfortable at the scrutiny.

After a few agonizing minutes, the woman returned the sunglasses to her face and clapped her hands again. "We have much to do."

Claire jumped again. She'd never get used to this.

The woman circled Claire and spoke as she walked, "First, we must address the main concern—your complexion."

Whipping her head around to catch the crazy lady's eyes, Claire asked, "What's wrong with my complexion? I've had it my whole life, and it's not something I can change. I'm not getting plastic surgery if that's what you're thinking."

The woman continued to circle. "No surgery. More fresh air and sunshine—or sunless tanner—something. You look sallow. No good. Second, we need to do something with your hair." She moved closer and lifted a lock of Claire's hair with one finger.

"What's wrong with my hair?" Claire had always liked her hair. She never did much to it, and she liked it that way. Other than the occasional trip to a salon to have it trimmed, she left it alone. Her mother had always said it looked like spun gold.

"Not wrong—but limp. Look at this." Mademoiselle Couture lifted another tendril and let it fall through her fingers. The piece of hair flopped on Claire's back. "See? Limp. We will restore body and life to it." She snapped her fingers, and one of her minions scurried over, carrying a notebook and a pen. Couture spoke several things in French to the assistant, who scribbled it all down furiously.

Claire picked up the end of her hair and inspected it while the two women exchanged words she couldn't understand. Hmm. Maybe she had a point.

Mademoiselle Couture walked around Claire again. She pointed to Claire's dress. "Also, we must do something about your attire. Now that you will become queen you must present yourself impeccably at all times. Never casual. Never frumpy."

Claire gazed down at her dress. She didn't see anything wrong with it. Besides, some assistant or helper or someone from the queen mother's staff had brought Claire her current wardrobe, supposedly approved by her grandmother. She couldn't believe this woman would say something against the queen mother's selections. Claire's eyes drifted to dog hair along the hemline. A speck of mud from her puppy's paws caught her attention. *Oops*. She hadn't noticed that. Okay, so she didn't look "impeccable," but how damaging could some dog hair and a hint of mud be?

The woman's eyes followed Claire's to the offending agents. She pointed at them with one finger. "You see. We cannot have anything out of place. I'll gather a brand-new wardrobe as well as some selections for the coronation day." She spun around and ceased her orbit of Claire, then strolled over to stand before the queen mother. "We'll need to schedule another time soon to try on things and allow time for tailoring. I'll have my hairstylist and makeup artist come along as well. I can have everything prepared in a few days, perhaps sooner. Would that be acceptable?"

The queen mother sent the small-but-mighty woman a smile. "That sounds fine. I'll have Albert arrange it. Thank you for your time."

Mademoiselle Couture curtsied and then clapped her hands for a final time and shouted to her staff instruction in French. Then, in a clatter of black stilettos, the room emptied as quickly as it had filled.

Her grandmother glanced at her. "That went well."

Claire muttered, "I'd hate to see what going poorly looks like."

Her grandmother murmured, "Hmm?"

"Oh nothing." Claire glanced at the watch on her left wrist. "I wondered if we might wrap up coronation lessons for today. I have a meeting at the hospital this afternoon, and I don't want to be late."

Her grandmother glanced at Claire and looked like she wanted to object, but instead placed her hands in her lap. "Very well. Let's try to get an early start for our next session. I'll have Albert confirm a time with Mademoiselle Couture. I want you to practice with the crown and scepter as well. It can be tricky walking with a larger crown than it looks, and we don't want any missteps on Coronation Day."

"No problem—but will she have all those clothes ready in a few days?"

Her grandmother dipped her head and narrowed her eyes. "What do you think?"

Claire chuckled. "Okay, you make a good point. She's a force. I'm sorry I doubted her. Well, I'd better go." She curtsied even though her grandmother insisted that she didn't require the formality. Claire found herself slipping into old habits from her early royal lesson days.

Her grandmother nodded and rang a bell next to her, calling for Albert.

The queen mother dismissed her. Claire rushed away before her grandmother could find something else royal to teach her.

The drive to the hospital would only take thirty minutes. Still, if she grabbed her planner and cell phone, she could knock out several items before she arrived at the meeting. The hospital charity wanted to hold a bigger benefit in a few weeks. Although they had an event planner on hand, Claire had a hard time letting go of responsibility. Her mother always said that if you wanted something done right, then do it yourself. It was still good advice.

Claire dashed upstairs and found her planner on her desk. She penciled in the next meeting her grandmother had planned with the fashion guru. Her eyes landed on her cell phone on the nightstand, and Claire retrieved that, too. Grabbing the handbag hanging from the doorknob, Claire clutched her planner to her chest and hurried downstairs.

On her way to the castle's front door, Claire kept her head down, running through a mental to-do list. She didn't notice the obstruction in her path. "Oof." Claire slammed into a tall body and knocked nearly all the wind from her lungs. Her planner went flying across the floor, and she and the human barrier landed on the ground in a pile.

A high-pitched voice screeched, "What is wrong with you? Do you ever look where you are going?"

Maurelle. Of course. Claire did not have time to deal with her today. *Try to be nice. Try*. "Maurelle," Claire spoke her stepmother's name in a smooth, even tone. *Stay calm*. "I'm sorry, I didn't see you there."

"Humph. I should say not. It's no wonder you ran me over the way you were staring at your feet and muttering to yourself. Queens do not walk around in such a state. I don't know how you'll manage to learn these things in a few weeks."

Claire pushed herself to a standing position and offered a hand to Maurelle to help her.

Maurelle fumed, "I can get up on my own accord. I don't need your help." She rose with such grace that while Claire should have been angry at the affront, she instead marveled at the hateful woman's poise.

The woman smoothed her black pencil skirt and crossed her arms in front of her chest. Her red nails gleamed from a fresh polish. "Where are you off to in such a hurry?"

Claire couldn't stop staring at the red nails. "Um, I have a meeting at the hospital—for charity."

"Ha! Charity. You don't have time for such things if you plan to be ready for your coronation and wedding. You're spreading yourself too thin."

Setting her jaw, Claire stood her ground. "I happen to think charitable acts are important, and I'm blessed to be able to help and use my medical skills. Please, don't trouble yourself with what I can and cannot handle. I appreciate your concern." *Yeah, right*. Her eyes darted around the floor until she saw her planner. She scooped it into her arms. "Now, I must go, or I'm going to miss the entire meeting. Have a good day."

Maurelle spun and strolled away without another word.

Claire bounded out the front door to the driver and car waiting below. *Yep, a good day. Just great.*

Chapter 8

Claire dashed to the elevator running in an unladylike manner that would have caused her grandmother to cringe. Her arms flapped in the air like a chicken, waving for the gentleman inside the lift. "Wait. Hold it, please!" The man stuck his arm between the closing doors, causing them to part and allow her to enter.

She hadn't bothered to look at the helpful stranger's face, focusing on trying to make her hospital charity meeting. Glancing at her watch on her wrist, she sighed. Five minutes late. Not good. Her grandmother always demanded punctuality, and now that Claire represented the royal family, she had to provide a good example.

Moisture pooled at the back of her neck and caused her white blouse to cling to her skin. *Super. Way to make a great first impression.* Dr. Wexford knew Claire, but this was her first time presenting herself to the entire committee. Today the committee would discuss plans for the upcoming charity event, The New Life Foundation. The event would raise funds to help patients and families who couldn't afford care. Her position at the foundation was supposed to be more figurehead in nature, but she liked work—better than speech-giving any day.

She dabbed her forehead with the back of her hand and shook her top away from her sticky skin. "Whew. It's hot today. Of course, all that running didn't help things. Thank you for holding the elevator for me. I've got a big meeting, and I'm already late."

"Yes, I know. I'm running a tad late myself. Good to see you again, Claire, or should I say, Your Royal Highness."

Claire's head whipped up, and her eyes landed on the stranger's face. *Richard. No way.* She hadn't recognized him at first because she'd been focused on her tardiness. What was he doing here? Was this some scheme to get back at his brother? She collected herself before responding, "Richard. How are you?" *How are you? What kind of ridiculous opening question was that? How about what sneaky plan do you have that involves my foundation, and how will this hurt your brother?*

He dipped his head. Wearing a charcoal suit and tie, he looked much older than his age. "I'm here for the same reason as you—to help the hospital and its new foundation." He sent her a crooked smile.

Claire didn't like to judge others. The Bible told her not to do it, and her mother had reiterated the same thing throughout her childhood. Still, she didn't trust him—not even a little. "Oh? What's your role on the committee?"

"Dr. Wexman asked my father to provide his business acumen and political connections to the foundation. He couldn't make it to today's meeting, so he sent me."

Claire's throat ached. No. Ethan's family despised her. All she wanted to do was use her medical skills and help others. Don't you want Ethan and his family to reconcile? Isn't that what you were saying to Granny the other day? Maybe this will be the opportunity for reconciliation.

Richard smirked. "I have to thank you."

The elevator's doors dinged and parted.

Richard made a show of spreading an arm before her, indicating she should go ahead of him.

Claire nodded and exited, thankful to put more space between them.

He followed behind her, whistling a tune.

She lifted her head and looked at him. "For what?"

"Hmm?"

"You said you wanted to thank me. For what?"

He sent her that knowing grin. "For taking Ethan out of the picture so I could have a shot at the top spot in the family. He never appreciated everything he had handed to him. Always the favored one. Always my parent's great hope." Richard chuckled. "Not anymore. Now, it's my turn. If he hadn't lost his mind and run away with you, then I wouldn't be the sole heir to my father's estate and preparing to marry Abigail Fulton. Her family's extremely wealthy—more so than the Crown."

Claire guessed this wouldn't be the happy family reunion after all. At least she'd talked her security detail into staying behind at the car. It had taken a lot of begging, pleading, and promising to go directly upstairs and return in the same fashion. She didn't need any witnesses to this exchange in case she slugged him. No— she wouldn't do that. *That's not Christian at all*. Plus, her mom would have disapproved. Still, Granny probably would be rooting for her on the sidelines. She giggled at the image.

"What's so funny?" He raised a brow and stopped at the conference room door.

She smoothed out her dress and tucked her hair behind her ears. "Nothing." Raising a hand, she grabbed the silver lever and opened the door. As soon as her foot entered the room, everyone seated around the large conference room table stood. The men bowed at the waist, and the women gave a small curtsy. Claire froze— she doubted she'd ever get used to the formality.

"Your Royal Highness, come in. Please take a seat. We've left the head of the table open for you." Dr. Wexman gestured toward the opposite end of the table.

She nodded. "Thank you. I'm sorry I'm late. Traffic was horrible, and well, there's no excuse. Please, accept my apologies." Claire hurried to her seat, but her grandmother's voice resonated in her mind. *Slow down. Walk with purpose. Head lifted, eyes straight ahead. Don't walk like a mummy or a wind-up doll.* She slowed her stride and made her way to the empty seat. Sinking into it, she breathed a sigh.

Dr. Wexman addressed Richard, "Good of you to join us. Your father's not coming?"

Richard shook his head. "He had another meeting he couldn't reschedule, but he sends his regrets." He walked to an open seat next to Dr. Wexman and settled himself into it as if he owned the hospital.

"Very well. If we're all ready, let's begin." He looked around the table. At least ten other attendees came to help with the planning the foundation's fundraiser.

Once everyone had retaken their seats, Claire's eyes drifted to the folder in front of her. She opened it and saw sheet after sheet filled with memorandums about the event and an endless list of items to accomplish. It was worse than she thought. She swallowed hard and did a quick mental calculation. Yep, if she didn't sleep for the next forty-eight hours, she might make all her deadlines.

"Dr. Thomson, or uh, Your Royal Highness, uh—" Dr. Wexman looked uncertain how to address her or proceed.

She waved away his formality. "Dr. Thomson is fine."

He picked up his glasses from the table and placed them high up on his nose, where they'd left a permanent imprint on his face. "Right. Well, as you can see, there is much to be done over the next few days. I realize the coronation is approaching, too—will you have enough time to devote the attention to this event it deserves?"

Claire had her doubts—big ones. Still, she pasted what a smile on her face. "Absolutely. No problem. I've got a few patients to see this evening after our meeting, but tomorrow is free. Where are we at with preparations for the event?" She shouldn't call it an event—a ball was more like it, and a big one at that.

"Most of the logistics for the event have been taken care of by my secretary. The other committee members have divided some of the tasks such as reaching out to our biggest donors to ensure their attendance and taking care of the guest list." He glanced at a paper in front of him. "However, I would like you to give a speech. Something about how crucial the hospital work is and how the foundation will benefit the community—things of that nature. Make it sound good. It shouldn't be a problem for Amorley's next ruler."

Claire pulled at the collar of her dress. *Why did they make necklines so tight? Was it getting hot in the room?* Perhaps, the thermostat had broken. Maybe someone could open a window or turn on a fan. Ugh—another speech. *Why did it always come back to public speaking?*

"Dr. Thomson?" he raised a brow and removed his glasses. "Will that be a problem?"

She gulped. "Not a problem." Claire reached across the table and grabbed the water pitcher on the table. Steadying her hand, she poured some into an empty cup in front of her. After taking a slow drink, she placed her cup down and resisted the urge to wipe her mouth with the back of her hand—something not future queen-like. *Not a problem at all—right?*

Chapter 9

Mademoiselle Couture clapped her hands together. "Ma'am pay attention. Time until the coronation remains short and you are off in another land. We still have to finalize your dress, accessories, and attire for the events during the week leading up to coronation. That week will be full of public appearances."

Claire whipped her head upward. "Public appearances?"

The petite dynamo narrowed her gaze. "Well, of course. What did you expect? You are about to be crowned the ruler of a major country. The world will be watching—always. How you present yourself is of the greatest importance. What you wear matters."

"Right. Okay. Well, I'm sure whatever you select will be great."

The Couture Crew, Claire's name for the fashionista's team, all paused, and one of them gasped.

Lifting her brow, Claire peered at the shocked one. "What? Did I say something wrong?"

The queen mother sauntered over and placed a gentle hand on Claire's upper arm. "Dear, we cannot simply 'pick out something' in a cavalier manner for your presentation to the world as Amorley's new queen. Everything must be perfect. Mademoiselle Couture is correct."

Claire peered at her watch.

Mademoiselle Couture squinted further. "Are we keeping you from something?"

"Uh, well, yes."

The woman looked aghast.

"I mean, no, not exactly. I have the hospital's event tomorrow night, and I'm supposed to give a speech, so—"

The fashion guru slapped her hand to her forehead. "Oh, this won't do. Why would you give me such short notice? I'm not sure I have anything—Eleanor, check on the third rack. Did we bring the navy shift dress with the coordinating blazer?"

One of the black-heeled assistants whirled into action, click-clacking her way across the room.

Claire heard the clatter of hangers whacking against one another while the girl sifted through items on the rack.

"Aha. Here it is." The girl raised it in the air in victory and rushed it over to Mademoiselle Couture. She shoved it in her boss's hands, appearing eager to be out of the hot seat.

"Wonderful." Couture inspected the ensemble. "Well, it's not perfect, but it will do." She flicked it toward Claire and gave a curt nod of her head. "Go try this on."

Claire's eyes widened. "Right now?"

Mademoiselle Couture tapped her foot. "Yes, yes. Hurry, we have much left to do."

Afraid of upsetting the militant style queen further, Claire grabbed the outfit and hurried to the makeshift changing room Couture's staff had erected upon their arrival. It looked like a giant black octagonal tent. She seriously doubted its structural integrity but didn't dare object to Couture's orders.

Claire struggled into the body-skimming dress and shrugged on the blazer quickly. She dashed back outside, impressed with her time and forgot the royal lessons her grandmother had taught her. She planted her hands on her hips and grinned. "What do you think?"

Another flurry of gasps ensued.

Claire straightened and cleared her throat. "I mean, I believe this will work. Don't you?"

The queen mother lowered her glasses and peered over the top of them as she tended to do and gave a nod of approval.

Mademoiselle Couture tilted her head and said nothing for a full minute. All of her helpers held their breaths. When she uttered, "Fine," they all exhaled as a collective. They jumped into activity, gathering more options for the coronation day and the week leading up to it.

Claire dashed back to the changing area to put on the top contender for her Coronation Day gown. She'd stepped into it and gotten her upper body in the bodice when she hit a blockade. The dress felt tight, and unless she took up the study of contortion, she wouldn't be getting the zipper up on her own anytime soon. "Ugh," Claire grunted and twisted, hopping around inside the black tent.

"Shall we send someone in to assist you?" the queen mother asked, her voice laced with concern.

"Oof," Claire muttered. "No, no, that's okay. I can get it if the zipper will—agh—" She fell over, taking down the changing room and several awaiting outfits positioned on the wireframe overhead with her.

The tent wrapped itself around Claire, cocooning her in several layers of shame and nylon. She closed her eyes tight, praying if she stayed like this long enough, everyone might go away out of boredom. Popping one eye open to ascertain the damage she'd done, Claire's gaze landed on her grandmother's face first.

The queen mother's face paled, and her jaw hung open.

Several members of Mademoiselle Couture's team covered their mouths with their hands.

Couture herself stood with her arms crossed in front of her chest, her face crimson. She opened her mouth as if searching for the right words, then closed it.

Claire opened both eyes and wracked her brain for what to say. After several seconds she shrugged. "Oops."

Mademoiselle Couture finally spoke, "Please learn how to dress and walk appropriately before the big day. We cannot have a similar debacle at the coronation—or the hospital charity event, for that matter." Her eyes drifted to the gown Claire had tried on, now twisted up with the changing tent. "Let's hope you didn't rip the gown on the way down." She cocked her head to the side and snapped her fingers to her staff. "Don't stand there— help her up and retrieve the gown. It's a one-of-a-kind creation—be careful." Then, she click-clacked out of the room.

Ten minutes later, Claire stood, free from the constraints of the tent and the gown. She'd changed into her still too tight clothing, but it was an improvement.

Claire turned to her grandmother. "I'm so sorry. Really. I don't know how that happened."

Her grandmother hadn't spoken a word since the entanglement.

Claire noted the tiniest quiver at the edge of the queen mother's mouth. It looked like her grandmother was attempting to conceal a smile.

The queen mother raised a brow and whispered, "No need to apologize to me—to Mademoiselle Couture, maybe. She looked upset, didn't she?"

Claire stifled a snicker. "Just a little bit."

"At least your granny wasn't here to witness it. Can you imagine?"

Considering this scenario, Claire paused. "You're right. It could have been ten times worse. Granny would have loved it, and she'd have tossed one-liners off to Mademoiselle Couture all afternoon."

"Woof, woof." Wilson's loud bark and click-clack of nails on the marble floor caused Claire to turn around.

Wilson wore his collar and leash, which flapped in the air untethered. He bounded toward her, grinning, followed by Albert, chasing after the puppy. "Get back here. Come puppy. Sir Wilson. Oh, would you listen to me?" he shouted various commands in alternating happy and aggravated tones.

Wilson ignored Albert's attempts and zig-zagged away from him.

Claire whistled, and Wilson froze. "Come."

The puppy trotted over to her side and sat down next to her. He scratched his ear with one leg and then returned to an obedient sitting position.

"Good boy." She patted his head and rubbed the spot behind his ear that he loved for her to rub.

Albert had stopped chasing the puppy and sucked in gulps of air. "I—don't—understand—why—he—listens—to—you—and—no—one—else."

Claire frowned and put her hand on her hip. "That's not true. He listens to Ethan and sometimes Granny. When he feels like it." She grinned. It was true. Wilson followed Milo's footsteps and had a mind of his own.

"My dear," Claire's grandmother called for her attention, "I didn't have an opportunity to tell you, but we have a meeting in an hour with the head of parliament. He wants to have a sit-down with you before Coronation Day, and with everything on the schedule in the coming weeks, I thought it best to get it out of the way now."

No. Claire's hands turned clammy. "Uh, do you mean Abigail Fulton's father? As in the father of the woman Ethan was supposed to marry?"

Her grandmother turned her attention to Albert. She rattled off a list of items for the evening meeting. She paused and flicked her eyes toward her granddaughter. "Hmm?" What was that?"

"Abigail Fulton. Are you saying her father is coming here to have a meeting with me tonight?"

Her grandmother raised her head and lowered her glasses a bit. "I am. I realize it might put you in an uncomfortable position, but that's the job. Many obstacles will cross your path as queen, and there will be challenging people you must get along with at times. Best to learn the lesson now." Then, she leaned her head closer to Albert and continued listing items for him to check.

The matter was closed. In one day, Claire had endured a hospital meeting featuring Richard Kane, nearly mummified herself in a couture and nylon tent, and signed herself up to have a dinner meeting with Abigail Fulton's father. *Top-notch day. Top.* Notch. She sighed and accepted her fate as she shuffled out of the room, calling for Wilson to follow. Claire didn't know how she'd get everything done and handle it on her own. She glanced at her puppy, wishing her life could be as simple as his.

~

Claire stared across the dining room table and watched as Mr. Fulton, head of parliament, carved the tiniest piece of meat with his knife and fork before taking a meticulous bite.

"Delicious. Thank you for inviting me to dinner, Your Majesty," he addressed her grandmother.

The queen mother gave a slight smile and then continued eating.

Claire lifted her fork to her lips and took a bite. She chewed thoughtfully, considering what to say. *Hey, remember me? Your daughter was supposed to marry my fiancé. Sorry about that, but anyway, yeah, right. Not exactly.*

"I assume preparations are underway for the upcoming wedding as well as the coronation." Mr. Fulton commented matter-of-factly.

After sputtering and nearly choking on her chicken, Claire pounded on her chest and grabbed a glass of water. She gulped it down and sat her cup in its place before responding to him. "Um, yes. We're more focused right now on the coronation, but I believe Albert and my grandmother sent out the Save the Date cards to the guestlist already." Claire picked up her fork and attempted to take another bite of her meal.

He nodded. "I received it. It's a formality for the head of parliament to attend important royal functions."

Claire's fork fell out of her hand and clattered to the table. "I'm sorry. I must have hallucinated. Did you say you planned to attend our wedding?" *Surely not. Wouldn't that be a lovely reunion*? She envisioned herself, Ethan, the Fulton's, and Richard at her wedding.

He began carving another tiny bite to consume. "That's right. We'll also be at the coronation. Lots happening in the coming months."

The blood drained from Claire's face. "Yes. Lots." She cleared her throat.

The meal continued with Claire, Mr. Fulton, and the queen mother taking bites, chewing, and making forced small talk. By the end of the meal, Claire had pushed the same spear of broccoli around her plate a thousand times. She placed her fork down and dabbed her mouth with her napkin. Tradition called for no one to leave the table before the queen mother. When she finished her meal, everyone else must, too.

Her grandmother glanced at her granddaughter and dipped her head. Sitting her utensils at the bottom of her plate, she indicated the meal had come to an end. Rising from her seat, she caught Claire's gaze. "My dear, I'm sure you're exhausted. It's been a busy day. Why don't you get some rest? Tomorrow you'll have another meeting with me and Mademoiselle Couture. I want you to practice with the crown and the scepter."

"Great," she chirped. Just great. Claire stood and gave a small curtsy to her grandmother.

The queen mother led the way toward the hallway, and Claire stepped in line behind her, followed by Mr. Fulton.

Wilson bounded down the hallway, grinning. His ears flopped from side to side, almost double the size of his head. He barked and jumped up and down upon seeing Claire.

She leaned down and patted his head. "Calm down, buddy. Settle down."

Her admonishment didn't weaken his resolve. When he noticed Mr. Fulton standing behind Claire, his head perked up, and he froze for a second before barreling toward the new person. More barking and jumping ensued.

"Agh," Fulton yelled. "He's relieved himself on my leg."

Claire's hand lunged forward to pull Wilson off the man. She examined the man's leg, and sure enough, the dog had dampened the lower half of the man's pants.

Wilson didn't look apologetic about his offense. He wagged his tail as he sat next to Claire. She bent down while still holding his collar. "You can't do that, Wilson. We do that outside. Remember?"

The dog lifted his head and tilted it. He didn't look at all like he recalled that rule and had no intention of instituting it now or any time in the foreseeable future.

Turning her head, Claire caught Mr. Fulton's eyes. "Excuse him, please. He's still a puppy, and when he gets excited, he sometimes does that."

He smoothed his suit jacket sleeves and straightened his collar, still attempting to retain a shred of dignity.

Something about the image of the official-looking man worrying about his suit jacket while his pant leg remained coated in urine caused Claire to nearly chuckle. She bit her lip to keep from laughing.

Thankfully, Albert appeared, saving the day. "Mr. Wilson, you must stop running off like that. Honestly, we must bring in someone to train him. He doesn't come when I call him."

Claire frowned. "I'm sorry."

"Astounding," Fulton muttered under his breath. "Well, I must be going now. I need to change." He took a few steps closer to the queen mother and bowed at the waist. "Thank you for dinner. I'll see you at the coronation." Giving a stiff nod to Claire, he quipped, "Good evening."

Forgetting all formality, Claire waved her free hand, still holding Wilson with the other one. "Bye."

The man hurried down the hall toward the front exit as if Wilson might come after him and take out his other pant leg.

Claire couldn't help it. She snickered.

Her grandmother peered at her. "It would help if you composed yourself. He's right, you know. We should look into an obedience school for Wilson." She turned to Albert. "Will you check on that for us?"

Albert bowed. "Very well, Ma'am." Then, he scooped Wilson into his arms—a feat at this point as it seemed every month the puppy added another ten pounds to his frame.

Claire righted herself and straightened her shoulders. "Sorry, Grandmother. I'll do better, I promise. Good night."

The queen mother dipped her head. "Good night." As Claire watched Albert struggled under the weight of Wilson. The queen mother followed behind him making a tsking sound. Claire smiled. She didn't think the dinner had gone well, but it had been a good night. Good 'ol Wilson.

Chapter 10

Ethan glanced at his watch. He had arrived at the hospital's foundation event half an hour early because he wanted to check on Claire. With everything on her plate regarding the charity function, coronation practice, and her job, he had hardly spoken to her in the last forty-eight hours.

His eyes caught her figure across the room as she entered. He sucked in his breath. Man, she is beautiful. I can't believe in a few months I get to marry her. It wasn't only her physical beauty that made him love her—she had the kindest heart and always helped others.

He lifted his hand in the air to get her attention.

She raised her head and saw him, sending him a smile. Claire finished greeting a gentleman by the door and then made her way over to him.

The royal family didn't favor public displays of affection. Still, Ethan couldn't stop himself from grabbing her hand and squeezing it. He leaned down, putting his lips close to her ear, brushing them against it as he murmured, "You look gorgeous. Stunning. I missed you." He pulled his head back and squeezed her hand once more.

Her face flushed crimson.

Good. He still could make her blush. "Are you nervous?"

She arched her brow. "You mean about giving the speech?"

"Yes, not that you should be—you'll do great." He smiled.

She sucked in a long breath and released it slowly. "I hope so…but yes, I'm nervous. I pray I don't fall on my way to the stage or forget what to say."

"You won't. I'll be praying and cheering for you." Ethan glanced around and noted the absence of paparazzi in their immediate vicinity. He took a chance and leaned in and pressed his lips to her cheek for a quick kiss.

"Thank you for everything. I should be able to handle this public speaking stuff by now, but it still makes my stomach churn."

"Hey, I told you—you don't have to do this alone."

Staring into his eyes, she opened her mouth. "I—"

"Well, I have to say, I'm impressed. I didn't think you would manage to pull this event together, you've done it. Good for you," Maurelle's voice dripped with insincerity as she sashayed next to the couple.

Ethan noticed Claire's shoulders stiffen. She turned to her stepmother. "Thank you, but I didn't do it on my own. I had help from the hospital foundation committee and—"

"Oh, I'm sure you did. Of course, there's still the matter of your speech." She narrowed her eyes and inspected Claire. "You are giving a speech tonight, aren't you? I can't say it would look good if Amorley's next ruler made an appearance and didn't say a few words."

"Well, yes, I am, but—"

An approaching figure caught Ethan's eye. *Oh no— not now—not here.*

Richard strode towards them with his usual swagger. He nodded to his brother and Claire. "Good to see you both." He turned to greet the queen. "We haven't met." He extended his hand. "I'm Richard, Ethan's brother. He probably hasn't mentioned me."

Maurelle lifted her forehead. "Oh? Why would that be the case?"

Richard tilted his head and sent his brother a half-grin. "Because I'm the better brother, and he's jealous of me." He leaned in closer. "Didn't you hear? He imploded his birthright. Gave all his status and position, not to mention his inheritance, to me along with his fiancé, Lady Abigail Fulton."

Maurelle looked like she'd eaten the proverbial canary. She interlaced her spindly, pale fingers together. "Really? Well, that's a shame, isn't it?" Her countenance didn't share this sentiment. She looked overjoyed at the news.

She tapped her red fingernails together and straightened her long frame. "I hate to break up this reunion, but I must go. I want to find a seat so I don't miss a word of your speech," she purred, her eyes fixed on Claire. Maurelle spun around and sauntered away, leaving a pall in her wake.

"Great," Claire muttered and met Ethan's gaze.

He took both her hands in his and gave them another squeeze. "Hey, don't listen to her. You can do this." He peered at his brother. "By the way, why are you here tonight, Richard?"

Richard tucked his hands into his pants pockets. "Oh, didn't Claire tell you? She and I have been working together on the hospital foundation. We'll probably be spending lots of long hours together over the coming months."

Claire darted her eyes between Richard and Ethan.

Ethan frowned and stared into his fiancé's eyes. He could feel the heat rise from his chest and fill his neck and face. "Is this true? Why didn't you tell me?"

"It is true, but it's not like that. I went to the foundation meeting the other day, and Richard happened to be there and—"

The head of the foundation, Dr. Wexman, joined the awkward family gathering. "I'm afraid I have to steal Dr. Thomson away. It's time for her speech."

Claire shifted her eyes between the two brothers. "Uh, okay." She tipped her head closer to Ethan's ear and whispered, "Listen, I'll explain later. Please, don't worry about it. I love you." Then, she followed Dr. Wexman to the front of the room and took the stairs to the stage.

Ethan followed her figure as she crossed the stage and took her place behind the wooden podium in the center.

Richard rocked back on heels. "Sorry. I didn't know I'd divulged a big secret."

Refusing to let Richard see how much he'd upset him, Ethan clenched his jaw and stared straight ahead to the stage. "No worries, you didn't. The coronation, charity, and wedding planning have kept us busy this week."

Richard nodded. "I'm sure there's a lot to do. Still, if your fiancé isn't filling you in on the fact that your brother is working with her—"

Whipping his head toward Richard, Ethan fumed, "What?"

His brother shrugged. "I'm just saying if she's keeping secrets from you, maybe you should take the wedding plans of the list. Might want to wait and see how things go." Then, Richard walked away whistling, his hands still in his pockets.

Ethan stared at his brother's retreating figure and fought the impulse to tackle him from behind like they'd done when they'd wrestled or fought as kids. He's messing with you. Ignore it. He glanced at Claire again.

~

Claire adjusted the microphone and cleared her throat before turning her attention to the crowd. "Um, good evening. Thank you for coming tonight and supporting the Oxmund University Hospital New Life Foundation. As many of you know, the foundation offers support to patients and their family members and provides care for those who might not afford it otherwise. As I share my gratitude for your generosity, dinner will begin."

The room looked toward the head table and the queen mother.

The queen mother took the first bite from her plate, signaling that dinner could officially begin.

The waitstaff began dispensing plates covered in fish or Cornish hens to the attendees.   The guests picked up their utensils, and the sounds of clinking glasses and utensils against china resonated throughout the room.

Claire glanced at her notes on the podium and then lifted her head again. "Every donation tonight will benefit patients and their families. The work the foundation conducts daily is crucial to the country and this local community and—"

A woman jumped from her seat near the front of the room; panic painted across her face. "Help! He's choking. Please, someone, help him."

"I'm coming." Without thinking about the remainder of her speech, Claire leaped from the stage. She landed on the floor with a thud—in heels, no less. Taking two seconds to ascertain if she'd broken her ankle, Claire hopped up and dashed to the distressed woman's table.

Tears filled the middle-aged woman's eyes. "Roger. Oh, Roger, hang on."

The portly man clutched at his neck with both hands.

Claire could tell he wasn't moving any air, and he hadn't made an attempt at a cough in the few seconds she'd been at his side. "Sir, can you breathe?"

He shook his head.

"I'm going to do the Heimlich Maneuver. Do you know what that is?"

He nodded.

"Is it okay if I help you?"

He nodded again.

"Okay. Stand up and hold still."

He obliged and rose from his chair.

Claire wrapped her arms around his waist, made a fist with her left hand, and covered it with the right one. She placed them below his rib cage and gave two forceful thrusts inward and upward.

A ball of Cornish hen flew out of the man's mouth and across the table, splattering against the back of a long, black mane.

Oh no. Please, no.

The ball of regurgitated food pelted Maurelle in the back of her head.

Claire's stepmother turned her head around slowly. Maurelle's face turned a crimson color that surpassed anything Claire had seen before—worse than anything one of her dogs had done to produce a similar shade on her stepmother's face in the past.

Not knowing what came over her, Claire opened her mouth and tried to smooth over the situation, "Uh, you have a little something in your hair." Her eyes flew to the table and landed on a black napkin lying next to the man's plate. She grabbed it and hurried over to Maurelle. "Here, let me get that for you."

Claire dabbed at the goo-ball that had pelted Maurelle, trying to remove the offending agent as quickly as possible. After two swipes, she'd gotten rid of most of it, although she wouldn't claim that Maurelle's hair looked pristine—far from it. What are you doing?

Her stepmother screeched, "That's quite enough."

Claire froze and tossed the soiled napkin under the table, trying to hide the offense. "Uh, sorry. I was trying to help."

"Let me tell you what you've done, you—"

The choking man came to Claire's rescue. "She's saved my life. That's what she's done. How can I ever repay you?" He pulled Claire into a hug and squeezed her tight while patting her back.

"Oof." She squinted her eyes shut, trying to catch her breath until the man released her. "That's okay. It's my job to take care of people. It was nothing."

"No way. If it weren't for you, I'd be gone. Kaput." The man lifted his glass and turned to face the rest of the crowd. "Join me in a toast to the future queen of Amorley and the woman who saved my life, Dr. Claire Thomson. Here, here."

Claire's cheeks warmed. "Seriously, you don't have to—"

Everyone joined in the chant, "Here, here." Then, the room erupted in applause.

After a few seconds of standing frozen in appreciation and embarrassment, Claire did a small curtsy and then hurried to take her seat at the head table between Ethan and the queen mother. A waiter pulled her chair back for her, and she sank into it, relieved to duck out of the limelight at least a little. Relief coursed through her that Granny had stayed home to rest tonight. Claire would never have heard the end of it.

Her grandmother leaned over and whispered, "I can't say that the prospect of having someone else's food catapulted into the back of her hair pleased Maurelle. However, I'm proud of you. The leap from the stage wasn't the most ladylike thing I've seen—we'll have to work on exits later this week, but still, well done."

Claire smiled and sucked in a deep breath on a positive note, she'd escaped finishing her speech. Everything would be okay. Right?

Chapter 11

Ethan pulled out his chair and sank into it. He still hadn't gotten used to his new office. His father had fired him after Ethan announced his feelings for Claire and refused to marry Abigail Fulton. Fortunately, he had a degree and several connections, so he didn't end up living on the streets. Michael had a friend in finance who needed to fill a vacant advisor position at Smith, Ryker, and Thomas Financial Group.

He had a secretary, which was helpful. She had stacked all incoming assignments and mail in a pile on the center of his desk in no particular order.

Shifting some papers to the side, Ethan settled his eyes on an official-looking document.

425 Plum Hill Road
Dorekshire, Amorley 22244
To: Smith, Ryker, and Thomas Financial Group
    Regarding your request for full payment on loan no. 24536, I am unable to fulfill this commitment at this time. Instead, I would like another extension, perhaps for an additional three months. At that time, I will have the remainder of the balance. Thank you.

Respectfully,

James Kane, Earl of Abbingdon

Another letter had been stapled to the back of this page.

Smith, Ryker, and Thomas Financial Group
425 Plum Hill Road
Dorekshire, Amorley 22244

To: James Kane, Earl of Abbingdon
Dear Sir,

It is our regret that we are unable to offer an extension on loan no. 24536. The balance will be due in full no later than seven days from the date of this letter. If you do not make the payment, we will turn the account over to the bank's delinquency department. My understanding is that you have used your home, estate, and land as collateral, so as you know, the bank would garnish those items, too. I regret to inform you of this news.

Sincerely,

Mr. Alexander Smith, President of Smith, Ryker, and Thomas Financial Group

Ethan's mouth hung open as he processed the information. His parents owed Smith, Ryker, and Thomas money—a lot of money—and if they didn't pay it in less than a week, they'd lose everything. Why hadn't his dad told him about this? Because I'm dead to him.

What should he do? Ethan dug his phone out of his pocket and hit the contacts button. He scrolled through and found his father's name. Letting his finger hover above the name for a few seconds, Ethan changed his mind and instead scrolled down to another name. Pushing the button, he waited while the phone rang.

"Hello?" his mother's voice broke through his thoughts.

Ethan cleared his throat. "Mother? It's Ethan."

"Ethan?" her voice lilted up, sounding hopeful. "I'm surprised to hear from you."

"I almost didn't call. I didn't know what to do, but I wanted to check on you and Father. Are you okay?" His eyes jumped to the daunting letter still in his hand.

"Everything is—" her voice trailed off, and weeping replaced her words.

It was true. His pulse quickened. "Mother. What's going on?"

"Your father would have a fit if he knew I'd told you, but maybe you can help. Your father's in trouble."

"What kind of trouble?" Ethan asked.

"Big trouble. Your father leveraged everything we own against a risky investment. It didn't pay off—he lost all the money he invested and then some. He took out a loan from a local financial company to make money back with another venture, but that one failed, too. Now, the loans are due, and if he doesn't come up with the balance in a week, the bank will take everything we own. All we'll have left is our titles."

Ethan ran a hand through his hair. "I don't know what to say. I'm so sorry. What can I do?"

"Well, don't tell your father I told you any of this. He's a prideful man, and even though he's handled the situation with you poorly, he'd never admit it. I didn't handle it well, either, but he's my husband, and I didn't know what to do. I'm sorry, Ethan—sorry I didn't support you and try harder to make your father see your side of things. Will you forgive me?"

"Of course, I love you. Father won't see it as me helping, though. He'll look at it as meddling."

"No, he won't because I won't tell him—not yet."

"Alright, well, how bad are things? Financially?"

"As I said, your father put everything up as collateral. Things are bad. He hoped that your brother would secure a marriage with Lady Abigail in three months, and her family's fortune would save us."

Ethan placed the paper on top of the stack in front of him and stared at the word loan. "I take it things aren't progressing between them, then?"

Her voice brightened, "Quite the opposite. They are getting along well, and marriage is in the future, but not soon enough—certainly not in a week."

"I see." He gazed out his office window and considered his parent's options. A ray of light shone through, illuminating the dust particles that hung in the air. An inkling of an idea tickled his mind. "Do you trust me?" he asked his mother.

"Of course, I do. Now your father, on the other hand—"

He didn't let her finish the thought. "Great, then don't do anything."

"What do you mean?"

"Don't pay the loan. Sit tight."

"Won't we default on it? The bank will take everything we have."

"Exactly."

"I don't see how that is helping the situation. That's the very thing we want to avoid."

"I told you to trust me. I'll take care of everything. I promise."

Her voice cracked, "O-okay. If you're sure about this."

He clenched his jaw. "I'm sure. I've got to go, but don't worry about anything."

"Alright. I love you."

Ethan's throat ached. "I love you, too. Oh, and don't tell Father we had this conversation. I doubt he'd have as much faith in me."

"Not a word," his mother agreed. "Goodbye."

"Bye, Mother." Ethan ended the call and slipped his phone in his pants pocket. Then, he opened his laptop and got to work. In order to save his entire family's estate in the next seven days, Ethan had a lot of work to do. Maybe if he succeeded, this would repair some of the damage between him and his father. Perhaps, they could be a happy family after all.

Chapter 12

Claire stared at the crown and scepter in her grandmother's hands and gulped. "That crown looks pretty big. Are you sure I have to wear that particular one on Coronation Day? It'll break my neck."

Her grandmother gave her a thin smile. "I assure you that it won't hurt you, and you are fully capable of wearing it. Moreover, it's a requirement. Every Amorley monarch has worn this crown on Coronation Day. It's tradition."

Heaving a sigh, Claire took a step forward, accepting her fate. "Okay."

The queen mother's smile widened. "Good. Now, Mademoiselle Couture will place it on your head so we can see what hairstyle might best suit you for the big day. Then, I want to see you walk with it because you must wear it on Coronation Day as you sit on your throne and exit the building. I won't pin it in place, so you must have impeccable balance."

Mademoiselle Couture stepped forward. She furrowed her brow and sent Claire a pointed look. "Impeccable."

"Yeah, yeah, I hear you. I'll be impeccable." At least I'll try. Claire sat down in the chair, awaiting her artificial crowning.

"Wonderful. Mademoiselle Couture, would you do the honors and place this on Claire's head?"

The fashion guru nodded and took the crown from the queen mother, lifting it with care. She raised it above Claire's head and then placed it gently atop her hair.

She should have worn a bun today. Then, if the crown slid backward, at least it would have something against which to rest—kind of like a doorstopper. Instead, her long locks flowed down around her shoulders, perfectly conditioned and slick as a slide. One wrong move, and the crown would fly off her head.

Afraid to move, Claire froze.

Her grandmother frowned. "Dear, you can't sit so stiff. Smile and wave."

Claire cautiously raised her right hand and fanned it back and forth, palm forward, the way the queen mother had taught her during royal lessons. She forced a tight smile to her lips. "How's this?"

"You like one of those automatons at the state fair," Granny's voice chortled, echoing across the room. "You know, the ones you put a coin in, and they spit out some advice about life or other such nonsense."

Claire turned her head slowly, afraid to knock the crown askew.

"Now you look like a creepy doll, turning your head all slow like that. Honestly, Mrs. Couture, I don't know how you expect her to sit, much less walk, with that thing on her head. There aren't any hairpins holding it together." Granny drew her mouth to the side and made a tsking sound.

Claire hadn't wanted to invite Granny to this session of coronation lessons for this very reason—she had no filter. None. "Thanks a lot. I always dreamed of becoming a queen who resembled a creepy doll or a state fair robot. Thank you."

Granny burst into laughter. "Awe, I didn't mean to hurt your feelings. At least the whole scene makes for good entertainment, right? The crowd won't fall asleep from sheer boredom like at most of these hob knob functions. Silver lining." She walked closer to inspect the crown better.

The queen mother took a few steps closer, closing the space between herself and Claire and her grandmother. Mademoiselle Couture remained by Claire's side. "Let's try adding the scepter and having you walk with them both." She stretched her hand, holding the staff forward, and waited for Claire to take it from her.

The twenty-inch ornate stick rod a golden orb at the top covered in a variety of colored gems. Red, green, and purple hues glinted in the sunlight that poured through the large windows in the room.

"This piece of jewelry has been in our family for hundreds of years. Every monarch has carried it on Coronation Day and had their painting done wearing this crown and carrying this scepter. Now it's your turn." The queen mother smiled and raised her brow, waiting.

Claire rose from her seat, moving at a rate of about one inch a minute. After an eternity, she made it to an upright position. Putting her arms out at her sides as if traversing a balance beam, Claire took a few steps forward, surprised at her ability to keep the crown on her head. Once she made it within arms-length of the queen mother, she stretched her hand out and took the scepter.

She did it. Now, if she could turn around and walk back to her seat, then this horrible travesty of a practice session could end. Claire took one successful step and smiled. On her third step, she heard a noise—faint at first—off in the distance. It sounded like—no.

"Woof, woof. Woof, woof." Wilson sprang into the room, probably on a mad dash from Albert once again. He ran straight for Claire and circled her once.

She held one arm to the side while the other one carried her fancy staff. "No, Wilson. Stop it. Sit down. Wait. Off," she rattled off every obedience cue she could think of to no avail.

The puppy circled Claire and then jumped on her.

"No. No. I'm going to—" Claire didn't finish her sentence.

Wilson knocked her over, sending her crown and scepter flying across the floor. His eyes caught sight of the golden staff, and they widened with interest.

"No, Wilson. Stop. You can't have that. Stay. Wait. Leave it." Again, no use.

Wilson bolted for the scepter, which to him probably resembled a stick. He scooped it up inside his jaws and clamped down hard. Turning around, he stared at the group. Lowering his head, he wagged his tail behind him, ready for a game.

Claire righted herself and put her hands up in a defensive position. "Wilson, bring that back. It's not yours." She waved with one hand for him to come to her. *Yeah, right*.

He took two steps backward.

Claire tried to ease closer. "Come on, stay right there," she cooed in a calm voice even though her heart pounded in her chest. Her grandmother was going to kill her. That thing was a million years old and worth a fortune.

The puppy backed up further and crouched down again.

Oh no. Claire had seen this stance before—he was going to run.

"No. Please stay." Claire lunged forward, reaching for the scepter or his collar.

Her sudden movement took him by surprise, causing him to shake the stick. In doing so, one of the gems fell to the ground. His eyes fixated on it, and before Claire could stop him, he ate it. Whole. All of it.

"No! Agh." Claire slapped her hands to her cheeks, wanting to crawl under the throne and hide.

"Did he…eat a stone?" her grandmother asked, all color draining from her face.

Wilson had dropped the jeweled stick to the floor during his expensive snack. He now sat perfectly mannered, wagging his tail and emulating the picture of obedience.

Claire met her grandmother's gaze. "Uh, he—"

Granny slapped her hand on her thigh. "He ate it. Woohoo. Never seen anything like it. I love that dog. Not a dull moment around him." She cackled, oblivious to the distress the situation had caused the queen mother.

Claire frowned. "Granny, please, this is serious. Those gems are old and priceless. What are we going to do?"

Granny quieted herself and planted a serious look on her face. She shrugged. "Only one thing to do. Wait."

Raising her brow, Claire looked at her granny. "For what?"

A mischievous grin spread across her granny's face. "For it to pass."

The queen mother's hand flew to her chest. "No. You can't be serious."

Granny nodded. "Afraid so. No other option unless you think this warrants surgery."

Albert caught Claire's eye and sent her an empathetic smile. Albert raised his hand. "If I may, Ma'am," he interrupted, turning to the queen mother, "but I can take on the job of assuring the crown jewels are, uh, returned to their rightful place."

The queen mother gave a wave and sighed. "Very well. Thank you, Albert. I honestly don't know how we'd manage Sir Wilson if it weren't for you."

Claire flashed a grateful grin and mouthed the words, "Thank you." The queen mother was right. If it weren't for Albert, she and Wilson would be toast. She reached down and picked up the damaged scepter and handed it to her grandmother. "Sorry. Again."

Heaving another sigh, the queen mother accepted it. "Why don't we quit our coronation practice for today. There's only a few weeks left, but I think my heart has taken all it can today."

Maurelle entered the room wearing a long black gown and heels. She must have been waiting in the doorway and witnessed the entire spectacle because she wore a pleased smile. Her stilettos pounded against the floor.

Claire shivered at the sound.

She raised a brow. "Finished already? I'd imagine you'd have more to do, what with needing to learn old Amorley."

Furrowing her brow, Claire stood straighter. "What do you mean?"

Maurelle put a hand to her cheek and widened her eyes. "Oh, didn't your grandmother tell you? You have to give your coronation speech in the old Amorley dialect. It's quite difficult to learn. Have you practiced?"

Claire looked at her grandmother. "Is this true?"

The queen mother stared hard at Maurelle. "It's not something I'm aware is a requirement for her to do. I don't recall her father or grandfather doing it."

Maurelle inspected her perfectly-shaped nails. "Yes, well, that's because they didn't do it."

The queen mother shifted her handbag, putting it higher on her forearm. "Then why should it matter if Claire does it?"

Maurelle grinned as if she had a secret she couldn't wait to spill. "It matters because she isn't from pure, noble blood. Her mother was a commoner. Therefore, according to the Constitution, Claire must give her speech in the old Amorley dialect to demonstrate her allegiance to Amorley. If she doesn't, then the coronation will be void, and Eric will be eligible to take the throne."

Granny shifted her weight and smacked her red lips together. "It sounds like a silly rule to me."

Maurelle closed her eyes and turned her face toward Granny and frowned. "It may sound silly, but it's true." She glanced at the large clock on the wall. "Well, I must be going. I came into the room because I heard a scuffle from the hallway. I wanted to ensure nothing terrible had happened." Her eyes landed on the damaged scepter and then settled on Wilson. "My, my, that scepter's in bad condition. It's not the one you're using for the coronation, is it?"

Claire tore her eyes away from the damaged staff. "Uh, yeah."

Maurelle shook her head. "Oh, that's unfortunate." She leaned closer. "Is it missing a gem?"

"Listen, Granny and I have to leave. As you pointed out, I have lots to do, so thank you for informing me about the dialect, language, whatever thing. I'll look into it." She curtsied to her grandmother. "Sorry about the excitement today." Turning toward her granny, Claire asked, "Do you want to come with me and work on some of the other plans—maybe take a quick walk, too?"

Granny had a twinkle in her eye. "I'd love to," she lowered her voice so only Claire could hear her, "as long as you promise to provide more entertainment."

Claire shook her head. "Let's hope not." Let's hope not. She didn't know how much more stress her heart could handle. A few weeks—not enough time to do it all—not enough time at all.

Chapter 13

Ethan stood behind Claire as she sat at the long table in the library. He stared down at the book that had captured her attention.

Claire slapped its cover with her hand and then looked up at him. Dust billowed out the sides of the thick book. "What do you think? Can I learn it all in two weeks? And cover my shifts at the hospital? And my charitable duties? And coronation lessons? And anything else my grandmother throws in as a necessary public appearance?"

He scrunched his nose. "Do you have to learn it all? I've never seen a book that big."

She cocked her head to the side and opened the book's cover. Shoving her thumb in the middle of it, she flipped through several pages. "Yep. Well, not all of it, just enough to fake it through my speech. I have to say things like, 'What an honor it is to accept the crown,' and 'I pledge my allegiance to Amorley and its people,' you know, the usual stuff. Think I can do it?"

He paused for a second before answering, "If anyone can learn it in two weeks, it's you."

His hesitation must have upset Claire because tears filled her eyes.

Placing a hand on hers, Ethan sat down in the seat next to her. "Hey, don't cry. It will be alright. If anyone has enough intelligence and strength to do all of this, I believe it's you."

She lifted her head and wiped a tear away with her hand. "But?"

"But you might have to let the rest of us help you with some stuff. You can't do everything yourself."

Another tear trailed down her cheek, and she wiped it away with her fingertips. "I know you're right. It's hard for me to trust other people to help. For a long time, the only person I could rely on was my mom and Granny. I got used to doing everything myself."

He rubbed at her tears with his thumb, tracing the contours of her cheekbone with it. "You can rely on me," he whispered, his throat tightening. He loved this girl—so much. He'd do anything to make her happy—even try to patch up things with his family, plan a coronation, and deflect attacks from Maurelle at the same time.

She exhaled a shuddering breath. "Okay. Maybe you're right." A hint of a smile tugged at the corners of her lips.

"I am." Ethan reached for her hand. "Now come on—we've got work to do."

Claire placed her hand in his and squeezed it.

He reached for the stack of papers she'd brought with her and opened the hefty, dusty book. "Where do we start?"

She pulled a pen out of her purse and took the cap off of it. Tapping it to her chin, she tilted her head. "I guess at the beginning. How do you say, 'Welcome, my fellow countrymen'?"

He sent her a half-grin and flipped through the musty pages. "Ah, here we go." Ethan provided the answer and watched as his fiancé went into full-on academic mode.

She scribbled his response in her notebook.

The pair of them continued working on the phrases Claire would need for her speech. Thankfully, the requirements for the address were brief, but the old Amorley language proved difficult.

Several hours later, Ethan slammed the book shut. "That's enough for today. Aren't you tired?"

Her tired eyes closed, and she rubbed them with her fingers. "Yes, although I should keep at it—but you're right, I'm tired, too. At least we got some of the speech written and translated. If I practice every day, I might pull it off."

He scooted his chair closer to her. "Hey, I talked to my mother the other day."

She raised her brow. "Oh, yeah? How did that go?"

"It went well. At work I noticed a paper indicating that mother and father were in trouble—they might lose the estate and all his investments. So, I called her."

Claire put a hand to her mouth. "Oh no. What did she say?"

"Father made some bad investments and that there is a loan due soon—within a week. She asked if I could help."

"Wow. That's terrible. What can you do?"

"I don't know," he answered.

Claire rubbed his hand. "You'll think of something."

He smiled. "Thanks."

Putting away her pens, Claire glanced at Ethan. "Did I tell you what happened to grandmother's dress? The one she wanted me to wear for the coronation?"

"No, what happened?" Ethan asked.

"When I fell the other day in that silly changing tent, I ripped the gown, and I don't know what I'm going to do about that. She wanted me to wear it. It's super old and has been in the family for a million years."

Ethan rose, picking up the heavy textbook. "Still, it's only a dress. Maybe the queen mother will understand, and you can pick something else."

"Maybe—or maybe she'll revoke my royal privileges and decide I'm unfit to rule Amorley. Can't I wear my scrubs? I'm happy with them. They always fit, they're comfortable, and they don't judge me."

Ethan shook his head and smiled.

She sighed. "I don't want to think about it today. I'll talk to Mademoiselle Couture and see if she can find a solution. That thought scares me more than telling grandmother."

Ethan chuckled. "I bet. She sounds tough."

Claire stood and placed her purse on her shoulder. "Yep."

"At least the charity event went well. You saved that guy's life. The hospital and your grandmother have to be happy about that."

"Oh, they were pleased. According to my boss, the article in the paper the next day was the 'right kind of publicity'. So, that's good. Did I tell you he wants me to plan another event? He mentioned hosting it the day before the coronation so we could tie the two together for promotional purposes."

He raised his forehead. "The day before the coronation. Won't that be too much for you to do? It sounds stressful. You'll have to plan an event and work on your speech and all the details for the coronation."

Claire rubbed her forehead. "I know, I know, but I hate to tell him no. I promised to help with the hospital and the charity. All the balls I'm juggling are hanging in the air—I hope I can keep them there, and they don't come crashing down." She chewed on her bottom lip. "Let's forget about this stuff for the rest of today."

Ethan brushed a loose strand of hair off her forehead. He cupped her face in both hands and tipped it upward. Gazing into her blue eyes, his heart pounded faster. "I love you and I'm proud of you. You'll do great."

She gave him a soft smile, and her cheeks flushed pink. "Thanks."

He lowered his lips and pressed them against hers, gently at first and then with more intensity. Ethan's mouth melted into his soon-to-be bride's. How did he get so blessed? Soon, he would marry the love of his life. They just had to get through a coronation and an ancient linguistics lesson or two for the next few weeks.

When he pulled away from her, she beamed. Claire lifted her hand to his cheek and rubbed his slight stubble. "I love you, too. How about we grab a coffee and take Wilson for a quick walk. I'm sure Albert would appreciate the reprieve from puppy duty."

He nodded and grinned. "Sounds good." Ethan carried the textbook and Claire's notebook for her.

Ethan reached for her hand and guided her out of the library. Hope filled his chest—he'd save his family's estate, help Claire handle the Coronation, and look forward to marrying her. Glancing at her sweet face again, he whistled a tune.

She tilted her head. "I don't think I've ever heard you whistle before."

He shrugged. "What can I say? I'm happy."

The pair headed off to find Claire's rambunctious canine, tucking away their studies and responsibilities for the day.

Chapter 14

"Voila!" Mademoiselle Couture wore an exuberant smile. "What is the expression? Good as new." The fashion advisor stood in Claire's bedroom holding the queen mother's iconic dress from a hanger high above her head. The gold and blue applique, Amorley's colors, glistened in the sunlight.

Claire stepped forward and reached a gentle hand forward, running her fingers along with the embellishments and seams. Not a fiber out of place. No trace of her debacle in the nylon changing torture chamber remained. She couldn't believe it. "How did you fix it? It looked terrible before. Beyond repair."

The woman continued holding the dress and shrugged with her free arm. "What can I say? I'm a genius." She giggled.

The uncharacteristic response caught Claire by surprise. This woman had a sense of humor, after all. She exhaled and smiled. Things were looking up—finally.

Claire's relief lasted ten seconds until Wilson worked his nose through the tiny crack in the bedroom door. *Why hadn't she closed the door? When would she learn?*

He ran into the room caked in mud from head to toe. His blond hair looked dark brown, and he bounced from Claire to Mademoiselle Couture, unsure of who to dirty first.

"No, Wilson. Sit. Stop that. Stay down. Down," Claire admonished her puppy but to no avail. He was improving during training sessions, but something as tempting as a clean bedroom and an ancient ball gown proved too irresistible for him. She tried one last attempt. "Sit. Please."

Surprisingly, Wilson sat. He whisked his tail back and forth like a windshield wiper painting the cream carpet with dirt. At least he wasn't jumping on them or the dress.

"Good boy." Claire leaned down and patted his head.

He caught her eye and winked.

At least Claire thought it looked like a wink. She whispered, "No, Wilson. Stay."

He took this plea as an invitation to let loose and tear across the room, heading directly for Mademoiselle Couture.

The woman, dressed in a black ensemble, raised the gown higher. Though the front of it might have escaped the puppy's advances, the dress had a five-foot train in the back. She stretched on her tippy toes and extended her arm so high Claire thought the poor woman might dislocate it. That's when she screamed, "Don't you dare. Don't even think about it. I forbid it."

No use. The scene might have been comical under other circumstances. However, given the upcoming coronation, an impossible to-do list, and the fact that the ball gown out-aged Claire caused her palms to sweat.

Mademoiselle Couture caught Claire's eye. "Here. Catch." The woman threw the dress high in the air in Claire's direction as the puppy jumped on her legs, basting them in streaks of grime.

Claire leaped to the side and grabbed the bulk of the fabric. The hanger flew off and across the floor.

Wilson heard the hanger hit the ground and stopped his efforts at winning over Mademoiselle. He dashed off in the direction of the noise.

Whew. Close call. Claire relaxed her shoulders and let the dress drop down a few inches, giving her upper arms a break. *Mistake. Big mistake.*

Wilson must have sensed that Claire let down her guard because he ceased all advancement on the clothes hanger and diverted his efforts toward her and the crumpled gown. In two seconds, he crossed the room, soared through the air, and knocked Claire and the dress to the ground.

From deep within Claire's chest, a guttural sound emerged, "No." *Too late.*

Claire, the puppy, and the dress got coated in filth. As his denouement, Wilson left his signature mucky pawprint in the middle of the front of the gown.

Claire dropped the gown and grabbed Wilson, then looked up at Mademoiselle Couture to gauge her reaction.

The woman's face burned crimson, and she crossed her arms in front of her chest. "Well, I don't know what we do now. Your misbehaved dog has ruined everything. You'll have to tell your grandmother."

The queen mother would be furious. This dress meant a lot to her. Everyone had worn it for coronation since the beginning of time. Claire swallowed hard. "Is there—is there nothing else you can do? Clean it, maybe? Somehow?" Staring at the soiled gown, Claire held little hope.

"I don't know what you expect me to do. I'm not a miracle worker." The woman scowled.

"Please. Try something, anything. I'll tell my grandmother if you can't fix it, but there must be a way. Please." She placed her hands together in a prayerful pose.

The woman threw her hands in the air. "I'll try. I'm not making any promises, though. We may have to find another dress, and you may have to tell your grandmother that you've destroyed hundreds of years of tradition."

Claire sat, still holding Wilson to her chest. "I understand. Thank you." She glanced at the gown sitting in a muddy, rumpled pile on the floor. "Could I ask you for one last favor?"

The woman rolled her eyes. "What is it?"

Claire raised a brow. "Would you mind taking the dress out of the room? I'm afraid to move. He might get away."

Mademoiselle Couture grumbled but took a few steps forward. She reached down and lifted the dress from the floor and shook her head. "Hundreds of years—I have no words." Then, she turned on her stilettoed heel and stormed out of the room, dress in hand.

Claire turned Wilson around so she could look at his face. He'd grown so much that holding or lifting him had become difficult. He'd probably outweigh her soon.

The puppy gazed into her eyes and smiled.

She shook a finger at him. "That was not good. I can't believe you did that."

He cocked his head to the side and inspected her for a second. Then, he leaned in and licked her cheek as if to ask for forgiveness.

Her resolve to stay angry with him weakened.

Another lick and nuzzle from his wet snout, and the remainder of Claire's fury dissipated. "Okay, okay. I forgive you. I don't know what I'm going to tell grandmother, though. You and I had better pray that Mademoiselle Couture can fix the dress. I doubt that the queen mother will be forgive you if she finds out what happened to her family heirloom."

He tipped his head to the other side as if to say he didn't understand the big fuss about some dress.

"I don't get it either, Wilson, but that's the way it is around here."

He nudged her again with her nose.

"Alright. Nothing else we can do about it today. How about I change my clothes and bathe you?"

He sent her a sidelong look.

"Yes, I said a bath. You need one. You're filthy."

He sighed and relaxed his shoulders, accepting his fate.

She sat him on the floor, changed her clothes, and waved for Wilson to follow her. "Come on. We have to get you washed before anyone sees this mess."

Wilson obliged and trailed behind her.

Claire shook her head. She didn't know how she'd find a vintage, one-of-a-kind ball gown two weeks before the coronation. Maybe she wouldn't have to— maybe Mademoiselle would come through. *Maybe*.

Chapter 15

The following week passed by in a blur for Claire. Between meetings for the coronation, planning the hospital charity event, and learning an ancient language, Claire hadn't talked to Ethan on the phone, much less seen him.

Her eyes darted toward Wilson.

He cocked his head and raised one brow.

"What? I'm doing my best. If I don't do this stuff myself, it won't get done."

Wilson stared back at her with a look of disapproval.

"I know. I haven't seen Ethan in ages, but he understands. I'm sure he does." Besides, he had a lot to handle right now, too. He'd seemed more worried than usual—almost as if he had a secret.

The puppy's eyes shifted to a tiny gnat floating around the room. He jumped and pawed at it, determined to capture the creature.

Claire shook her head. "I'm glad to see you're so concerned." She glanced at the pile of books she'd been studying for her coronation speech next to the stack of items demanding her attention for the charity event and sighed. Digging her phone out of her pocket, she found Ethan's name in her contact list.

The phone rang three times before his recording informed her that he couldn't answer the phone and to please leave a message.

"Ethan, it's me. I'm sorry I missed you. I've been up to my eyeballs in language lessons this morning and wanted to see how you're doing. I miss you. It feels like ages since I saw you. Call me when you can. Love you. Bye." She tucked the phone away and promised herself she'd call him again later.

Wilson turned his head toward her and frowned—or at least it looked a lot like a frown. She didn't know dogs could do that. "What?" She tossed her hands in the air. "I tried. He didn't answer. I'm sure everything's fine. He'll probably call me back in a little bit. In the meantime, we have a lot to do. Starting with attending a meeting at the hospital to finalize the details of this charity thing. Which means—"

The dog sunk to the floor as if he suspected her following words.

"—that you have to go with Albert. Please, be on your best behavior today. No more mud. No more digging. No more jumping on people. No more destroying timeless heirlooms. Just run in the yard and find sticks. Okay?"

The dog's forehead raised, and his eyes widened. It didn't look like he'd agreed to the rules.

"Wilson, I mean it. Oh, and, whatever you do, leave Maurelle and Mademoiselle Couture alone. Let's not give them another reason to dislike us." She walked over, scratched the dog behind his ear, and then patted her leg, signaling for him to follow her.

The puppy grudgingly obliged, raising himself from the floor and stretching out each hind leg before falling in line behind her.

Claire grabbed her planner, her purse, and a stack of papers from her desk. Then, she turned off the light and headed out the door.

~

Claire stared across the table in the hospital conference room and locked eyes with Richard.

He smirked and then scribbled something on a notepad in front of him.

She shifted her gaze to Dr. Wexman. "I don't know how you can expect all this to get done so soon." Claire peeked at her phone to see if Ethan had returned her call. *Hmm, no messages. That's strange.* It was afternoon. He usually phoned her twice by this time of day.

Dr. Wexman spoke, pulling Claire's attention back to the conference room and the current conversation. "You promised to help with this event. I realize it's planned for the day before the coronation, but we must have your input. Also, you'll need to say a few words. The fate of the hospital and its patients depends on events like this. Remember, you promised that in exchange for hospital privileges, you would help promote the hospital. Have you changed your mind?"

Claire waved off his concern. "It's nothing like that. I have a lot going on right now. Of course, I care about the hospital and the charity. I want nothing more than to help the facility and its patients. It's fine. I'll do the speech and reach out to a few more potential donors to attend the event." *Along with the other fifty million things I have to do like, oh, taking an oath to protect and defend Amorley's interests in a billion-year-old language.*

The head of the hospital nodded his head. "Good. Glad to hear it. Also, let's focus on continuing to create only good publicity. The choking incident at the last event worked in the hospital's favor with the news, but let's aim for an uneventful event this time."

Claire's eyes widened. "I wasn't trying to create any kind of publicity when I saved that guy. He was choking. I didn't plan it and couldn't have avoided it."

The man tilted his head and steepled his fingertips together. "Still."

Still what? Should she have foreseen that the stranger would choke on his chicken or guinea fowl or whatever pheasant-type bird had been prepared for the fancy-shmancy event? Should she have ignored him and let him die? No, certainly not. She sighed. Sometimes, Claire didn't understand people. The weight of the upcoming events pressed on her shoulders. There were only a handful of days until the charity event and the coronation. Not much time.

Instead of unloading her opinion upon Dr. Wexman, she pasted a smile on her face. "I'll do my best to avoid an international incident."

He ignored her sarcasm. "Good. You do that."

The rest of the meeting zipped by, and as Claire added the fifteenth item to her to-do list, Dr. Wexman concluded the discussion, "That's all for today, people. Thank you for your time."

Claire stopped writing and lifted her head. Had the meeting ended? She couldn't focus. Ethan still hadn't responded, and usually, that wouldn't cause concern. Still, for some reason, today, she had a sinking feeling about it. Placing the cap on her pen, she gathered her things, and stood up, hoping to avoid a chat with Richard.

He'd positioned himself by the exit, obstructing her escape.

Too late.

"How are the coronation plans going, Your Royal Highness?" he bathed his words in disdain, and his announcement of her title didn't sound genuine at all.

She pulled in a breath before responding, "Fine. Great." They were not, in fact, great, but she wouldn't tell him that.

He shoved his hands in his pants pockets and leaned against the doorframe.

No escape.

He smiled. "Good. Glad to hear it. I guess you heard about the problems with Ethan?"

Claire furrowed her brow. "What problems? Ethan's fine."

He raised his forehead. "Oh, don't you know? He's in a meeting right now with Abigail Fulton's father and my father. Abigail didn't know what the meeting was about, but it must be important for him to meet with the two of them. I'm surprised he didn't mention it to you."

"I'm sure he was going to tell me about it. We've both been busy with the coronation and the upcoming wedding—lots to do."

Richard's face clouded. "Right, right. The wedding. For both of our sakes, let's hope Ethan hasn't changed his mind."

"Changed his mind about what?"

"About you…about the wedding. I wouldn't be shocked to find out that Ethan went back to Abigail. I tried to make her happy, but she broke up with me a few days ago. Said she didn't love me and couldn't marry me. Maybe she still has feelings for Ethan."

Claire's throat tightened. "How could she have feelings for him? They didn't even really date." At least, that's what Ethan had told her. The marriage idea between the two of them had been his father's plan.

Richard shrugged. "Maybe you're right. I bet the three of them discussing how sorry they are about how things worked out and asking why they can't be friends. That makes more sense than my brother decided to marry Abigail to save our family. You know my family's broke, right? Did he tell you that new piece of information? Flat broke. Dad lost everything. If Ethan or I don't marry Abigail, then my family's sunk. Since she doesn't want me—"

Claire lifted a hand to stop him from finishing his sentence. "I can't talk about this right now. I have a lot to do. You're wrong. Ethan would never do anything to hurt me. Never. I don't know what their meeting is about, but I'm sure he still intends to marry me." Tears filled her eyes. *Don't cry—not in front of him.* She clutched her planner and papers tighter to her chest and shouldered her way past Richard.

Richard called to her as she hurried away, "Hey, don't blame me for my brother's failings. Have a good day, Your Royal Highness. See you at the charity event."

Claire ran for the elevator and jabbed at the down button with his parting words ringing in her ears. The lift arrived, and the doors parted. She jumped inside and waited for the doors to close. Holding back tears, she rode down alone, and as soon as the doors opened, she burst out of the suffocating box.

Once outside, Claire sucked in fresh air. She fished around in her purse for her sunglasses, though the overcast sky with its dark clouds didn't demand them. Now hidden behind the black shades, tears filled her eyes. Hopefully, no media had followed her to take a picture of her current breakdown.

What if Richard was right? What if Ethan had been acting funny because he didn't want to tell her it was over, and he'd gone back to Abigail and his family. Claire walked down the street and darted into a small ally, giving in to a long cry. As wracking sobs took over her body, she wept for all that she'd lost in the past and her doubts about the future. She might have to lead Amorley alone—without her father's wisdom for guidance, her mother's arms for comfort, or Ethan's love.

Chapter 16

Ethan stared at his phone. *Claire.*

"I hate to rush off, but I have another appointment." Abigail extended her hand, palm facing downward in a dainty manner.

Ethan pulled his gaze away from the screen. "Oh, yes, you, too." He took her hand in his and gave it a gentle shake before releasing it. She turned and sauntered away as his phone buzzed again—probably a voicemail from Claire. He wanted to check it, but this meeting with his father and Mr. Fulton would not end. After an hour, his father had stormed away and left Ethan alone with Abigail's father. If they could come to an agreement about the merger, then he could step outside and return her call. His heart ached to see her.

He turned to face Mr. Fulton. "Can't we find a middle ground? You must see what an advantage my father's estate and expertise would provide to your company as a part of your investment portfolio."

Mr. Fulton rubbed his chin. "This could have all been avoided if our families had unified. Promises were made and broken—by you."

Ethan shifted uncomfortably. "I regret any upset and disappointment that I caused you or your family. I can't help who I love, and I love Claire, but because things didn't work out with Abigail and I doesn't mean my family's business couldn't benefit you. You would get forty-nine percent share in the estate and all its holdings, as well as my free expertise, and my family gets to keep its land and house. Everything we produce will directly benefit you."

Mr. Fulton frowned. "How do I know I'm not investing in forty-nine percent of nothing? Your father nearly defaulted on his current loan. How do I know he won't do the same to me?"

The man presented a valid concern. "Because even though I didn't marry your daughter, I am a man of my word. If I had known my father's business was in trouble, I would have helped him. He didn't tell me. Things between us haven't been good."

Mr. Fulton's face relaxed a bit and he nodded. Seconds passed before he answered, "Give me a little time to consider this proposal."

Ethan exhaled. At least he hadn't immediately said no. "Absolutely. However, my father's loan is due in a few days, so I need an answer by the coronation."

Mr. Fulton crossed his arms in front of his chest and stared at his feet before meeting Ethan's gaze again. "How about this? I'll have my answer by then, and I'll let you know at the coronation."

Ethan's eyes widened. "The coronation?"

"Yes. Didn't the queen mother or Dr. Thomson tell you I'd be in attendance? With my position in parliament, I must attend."

"Of course. Alright, then Coronation Day it is. Thank you for your time and consideration of the proposal, especially considering everything that happened in the past."

Mr. Fulton reached his hand forward. "I'm not an unreasonable man, despite how your father or the press might paint me."

Ethan shook his hand and held hope that he could repair things between himself and his father for the first time in months. Perhaps, Fulton would salvage Ethan's family's fortune. "Thank you for your time."

The man pumped Ethan's hand. "You're welcome. Now, I have to leave—I've got another meeting at my office this evening."

Releasing the man's hand, Ethan smiled. "Of course." He watched as Mr. Fulton walked away, carrying with him the last shred of hope for the Kane family's survival. Perhaps if Ethan could fix his family's financial problems, then his father would forgive him. Even though he did the right thing by turning down Abigail to propose to Claire, he hated what the decision had done to his relationship with his parents. This could fix everything. He sent a silent prayer to God to work things out and left for his office. He still had a lot to do in the next few days if he wanted to rescue his family's estate.

~

Granny twisted her lip to the side. "Hmm. Not answering?"

"No, but I'm sure he's busy with work. He's had a lot of meetings lately." At least that's what he'd told her in a text the day before. *Stop it. Don't let your mind run away with you. Ethan loves you. Besides, you have enough things on your plate with the charity event and the coronation. Focus on that.*

Granny made a tsking sound. "I don't like it. I thought that young man was helping you with learning that foreign language and plan your wedding. Not to mention your coronation is in a few days."

Claire bustled around her bedroom, a ball of nervous energy. "Well, he has things to do, and I'm a big girl. I can handle this stuff myself."

"Humph. I've heard that before. Look how stressed you are right now. There's a little line forming in the middle of your forehead. You're too young for that little line. It's too much. All of this is too much. You can't prepare for a coronation—whatever that entails—learn to speak Ye Olde Amorley and throw the hospital shindig in the next few days."

Claire rubbed at the alleged line on her forehead, willing it away. "It sounds like a lot, but if I stick to my schedule, which is written out in my planner, then—"

Her granny jumped up from the edge of Claire's bed. "Ha! I knew it. That silly planner—it's the root of all your problems. Let the plan go and ask for some help or let something go. Why don't you tell the hospital you need a break and can't make the charity event? I'm sure they'll understand."

Claire paced back and forth, wearing a path in the plush carpet. "I'm sure they won't. I have to do it—I promised. Besides, that is the least of my problems. I still haven't figured out what I'm going to wear to the coronation or how to tell the queen mother that I ruined her beloved gown."

Granny gave a low whistle. "What are you going to do? She's not going to be happy about that."

Claire sent her granny a sidelong stare. "No, she's not. That's why I've put it off this long. I hoped that

Mademoiselle Couture would work a miracle and restore the dress."

Granny guffawed and doubled over. "Restored? Did you see that thing? In my time, I've seen your dogs do some damage, but what Wilson did to that coronation gown beat it all."

Pressing her lips together, Claire turned to face Granny. She stopped pacing and planted her hands on her hips. "Thanks. Super helpful."

Raising her palms in defense, Granny shook her head. "Hey, I'm not saying that I'm happy about it—I'm only stating the facts as I see them. What's the dress backup plan?"

Claire plodded across the room and sank onto the bed next to her granny. "Oh, I have a dozen options that Mademoiselle's team dropped off earlier this week. They told me to pick something days ago so they would have time to select accessories for it." Claire chewed on her fingernail. "I stalled, praying that I wouldn't have to tell grandmother, but there's no other way. I have to do it."

Granny slipped a frail arm across Claire's shoulder and squeezed it. "It'll be okay. Tell her and get it over with—it's just a dress."

Claire snorted. "That's what you think. Nothing around here is just a dress. Everything's some long, lost, family heirloom."

Granny shrugged. "Still, it's a dress—not the end of the world. Also, I'll help you study. You have the charity event tomorrow night, but we have the rest of today. I've seen you buckle down and learn twice as much in a day preparing for medical boards. This Amorley language thing will be a breeze."

She rested her head on her granny's shoulder. Gratitude filled Claire's chest. "Thanks, Granny. I love you."

"I love you, too. Now, come one. Let's crack open some books."

The pair rose, and Claire gathered her planner, books, and papers, ready to study. Claire followed her granny down to the study, thankful that she could always count on Margaret Thomson.

Chapter 17

The day of the charity event brought uninterrupted chaos. Between finalizing her opening remarks, cramming for the coronation speech, and making a dozen last-minute decisions, she'd forgotten to eat breakfast and lunch. Claire glanced at the clock on the nightstand in her bedroom. 2:00 p.m. She'd never make it until dinner if she didn't eat a snack.

Pushing herself away from the desk, Claire hurried out of her bedroom. She took the stairs to the kitchen, where Albert awaited. He had grown accustomed to her lapse in a dietary schedule as of late. Thankfully, he'd left a basket filled with her favorite snacks in the pantry. The queen mother hated when she didn't sit down to a proper meal. Still, given all the preparations for the coronation, charity event, and wedding, she'd let it slide recently.

Claire's stomach growled. Her hunger distracted her, and she didn't notice the obstacle in her path until she slammed into it. "Ouch."

"Would it be possible for you to watch where you're going for once? Do you always walk around staring at the floor?" a disdain-filled voice dripped with disapproval.

Claire froze. *Maurelle*. "I'm sorry, I didn't see you there.

"Hmm. Pay more attention next time. Why are you in such a hurry?"

"Oh, I was on my way to get something to eat. I've been so busy I missed breakfast and lunch."

She arched a brow. "Oh? I thought you'd seen the newspaper article and gone on a mad dash to hide in your room."

Claire scrunched her forehead. "What newspaper article?" *Not again*. It couldn't be about her and Ethan because they hadn't seen each other for several days.

A sneer spread across Maurelle's face. "The one about Ethan Kane and Abigail Fulton. There's a photograph of the two of them looking cozy. Did you know he went to see her?"

Claire shook her head.

Maurelle's mouth formed a small circle. "My, my, well, it sounds like the pair of you have a lot to discuss. Of course, I'm sure there's an explanation for why your fiancé would meet his previously betrothed and not tell you." She started to walk away but paused. "The photo does appear a little incriminating. He's holding her hand, and there are only inches separating them. It looks— well, why don't you see for yourself. There's a copy of today's paper on the dining table." Maurelle spun around and strode away, her head held high.

Her stepmother hummed under her breath as she retreated.

Claire didn't know what surprised her more—that Ethan had met with Abigail and not told her or that Maurelle could hum. The concept of producing a joyful noise of any kind should have escaped that woman.

Why didn't Ethan tell her about meeting with Abigail? *It's probably a misunderstanding. Don't panic.* She recalled the missed phone calls and days apart from Ethan. Claire's heartbeat quickened and she rushed off toward the dining room.

The newspaper lay on the table, taunting her. She walked to it slowly and picked it up, closing her eyes and drawing in a breath. When she opened her eyes, Claire's stomach plummeted. *No. It couldn't be true.*

A picture of Ethan and Abigail Fulton standing inches apart filled half of the front page. Ethan held Abigail's hand and had leaned in as if to share a secret with her. They looked like more than friends. She slammed the paper on the table and spun around. Hugging her arms around herself tightly, Claire clamped her eyes shut, forcing down tears.

Stop it. Don't overreact. Claire trusted Ethan, didn't she? He would never hurt her. When she opened her eyes, the queen mother stood at the doorway.

The queen mother clasped her hands together in front of her and stood tall like a statue.

"I take it you've seen it?"

Claire's throat ached. She swallowed hard against the knot forming and replied with a slight nod.

"Is there something going on between the two of them?" her grandmother asked.

Claire shrugged.

"Well, the timing couldn't be worse. We have the hospital charity event tonight and tomorrow is your coronation. How are we going to explain this picture to the press? Ethan's garnered himself a reputation after the last photo they printed of the two of you." She sent Claire a pointed stare.

"I know it looks bad, but I told you the last time nothing more had happened between Ethan and me, and I'm sure this time is the same—an opportunistic journalist taking a photo at the right moment to make Ethan look bad. Scandal sells."

The queen mother walked closer to Claire and stopped in front of her. She removed her glasses and let them hang from her neck on a chain. "Have you talked to him?"

"No. I haven't. I called him several times yesterday, but he had told me he would be in meetings all day—that it was something important. He hasn't called back—but he will."

"Hmm. Let's hope so. The Crown cannot afford a scandal so close to your coronation. Maurelle or Parliament could complain that if your engagement is at risk, you aren't a suitable candidate for the throne. Stability is crucial.

Granny entered the room wearing one of her classic ensembles—a purple tracksuit, the gold necklace with the rhinestone ball, and orangey-red lipstick. "I don't see why Claire has to follow such an archaic rule. She could lead a country as a single woman—she's strong."

Pressing her lips together, the queen mother lifted her glasses and placed them on her nose. She glanced at Granny and surveyed her outfit. "Hmm. Well, I agree with you, but unfortunately, I don't make the rule. It's part of the Amorley Constitution, and Claire knew her engagement remained part of the stipulation. Suppose the press, Parliament, or Maurelle suspect trouble in your romantic relationship. In that case, they will latch on and not let go of the information."

Claire lifted her eyes and met her grandmother's scrutinizing gaze. "I'm sure there's an explanation." She reached for her purse and dug out her phone. Pulling it out of the bag, she called Ethan. Claire's fingers trembled. *What if it was all true? Had he been lying to her this whole time? Could she count on him? Trust him?*

The phone rang several times, and then Ethan's voicemail told her that he couldn't take her call right now and to leave a message. The phone beeped. Under the scrutiny of her grandmother and Granny, Claire spoke, her voice shaky, "Uh, Ethan, it's me. Claire. Uh, I don't know if you saw the newspaper today, but I need you to call me back. It's urgent. Okay. Bye." She pushed the red end button and returned the phone to her purse.

Granny narrowed her eyes. "No answer?"

Claire shook her head.

Granny clapped her hands together, commanding everyone's attention. "Well, I say we march over there and get to the bottom of this. Either it's a simple excuse, and there's no funny business, or that young man is going to have to deal with me." She pointed at her chest.

Something about the idea of Granny setting straight Ethan—a tall, strapping man—made Claire chuckle.

The queen mother took Claire's hands in hers. "Dear. You must be upset, but there's little time. Please find Ethan and see what happened. I'll call the press secretary and have her give a formal statement denying anything being amiss. Then, Mademoiselle Couture will come by and help you dress for the charity event. We will ride over together in the limousine tonight. Hopefully, by then, you'll have sorted out this mess."

117

Claire sucked in a deep breath and released it. "Okay. I'll head to his office first. Maybe he's swamped with work."

Granny stood straighter, though she still had a slight bend in her spine from years of arthritis. "I'm going with you—in case you need back-up."

This image caused Claire to laugh out loud. After a few seconds, she regained her composure and gave a big sigh. "Oh, thanks, Granny. I needed that. Alright, come with me. You're right—I might need backup, especially if Abigail Fulton is there."

Granny looped her arm in Claire's. "You got it."

The queen mother led the way out of the dining room, and Claire and Granny followed behind.

A wave of apprehension coursed through Claire. She prayed Ethan would calm her worries but couldn't shake the feeling that something big had happened and he'd kept it from her. *Only one way to find out—track him down and ask him.*

~

Claire raised her hand to knock on Ethan's office door and paused. What if she found out something she didn't want to know? No, she had to find out the truth. *Pull it together.* Tapping on the door with her knuckle, Claire waited.

After a few seconds, she made a second attempt. Still no answer. Claire turned around and looked into her granny's eyes. "I guess he's not here."

"Why don't you call him again."

She nodded and pulled her phone out once more. Thirty seconds later, Claire still had no answer from Ethan and decided not to leave another message. She had her pride, after all. "Nope. Not there. Now what?"

Granny tilted her head. "Well, there's not much else we can do at the moment. Let's head back to the castle and prepare for that charity hoopla thing you have tonight. I'm coming, too. I don't want anyone else messing with my granddaughter today. If I'm there, I can keep everyone in line."

Claire sank on the front step. She slumped forward and rested her forearms on her knees. Hanging her head, she sighed, and tears filled her eyes. This time, she let them spillover, and a sob escaped her lips.

Her granny sat down next to her. "Ooh, this stair is hard. How can you stand it?"

Raising her head, Claire swiped at a tear. "That's what you're thinking about right now?"

Granny shrugged. "What can I say?" She patted her granddaughter's back. "It's going to work out—I promise. Remember, it's the Thomson girls against the world. No matter what, I'm here for you, and I believe Ethan's a good guy. Don't jump ahead of yourself—wait and see what he says."

Nodding, Claire buried the rest of her sobs. "You're right. I guess there's nothing else I can do about it right now." She pressed her palms against her knees and stood. Reaching her hand down, Claire helped her granny stand, too.

Granny rose slowly and groaned. "These old bones are aching more and more each day." Once upright, she clutched at her chest.

Claire frowned. "Are you okay?" Her granny usually acted tough. She had such a young and spunky spirit that Claire often forgot her granny's age. "Should we head to the hospital?"

Granny swatted at the air with the other hand. "No, no. That's nonsense. I'm fine—I need to catch my breath, that's all." After a few seconds, she straightened and pulled in one more deep breath. "There. I'm good."

"You're sure?" Claire raised her brow.

"I'm positive. Come on—let's get ready for this shindig. I wonder who'll choke on chicken or have a medical emergency tonight? Maybe you can save the day again. That would teach the press a lesson or two. They'd have nothing but good news to print."

"Oh, let's not wish anything like that. I'm praying the whole thing goes smoothly, and I make it through my speech without forgetting it or tripping. Then, I need to figure out what's going on with Ethan and prepare for tomorrow."

"Alright, let's go." Granny led the way to the limousine and hunched down, sliding inside.

Claire followed behind her granny and whispered a prayer that everything would work out well—hopefully, she could talk to Ethan soon and he'd explain the reason for his meeting with Abigail. Perhaps she could survive the night without any more scandal. *Hopefully.*

Chapter 18

Ethan frantically scanned his apartment. It had to be here. He'd had it during his meeting with Abigail and her father. He'd checked it and seen that Claire had called. After that, he thought he put it in his pocket. Then, he'd returned to his apartment to pick up his suit for the charity event and headed to his office. When Ethan got to the office to grab some papers, he couldn't find his phone. Dashing back to his apartment, he had searched every room, drawer, and shelf—still no phone.

He leaned down and looked under the bed one more time—nothing other than a few clumps of dust and a lone sock. Lifting his head, Ethan glanced at the clock on his nightstand. Five p.m. The charity event started in one hour. He'd run out of time for the phone search—he'd have to do without it. At least Claire would be at the dinner, and he could talk to her there.

Resigned, Ethan hopped in the shower and shaved. He threw on a dark charcoal suit and black dress shoes. After a few swipes of gel through his hair, he grabbed his watch, keys, and wallet and walked out the door.

He locked his front door and hurried down the stairs to his car parallel parked on the road. Ethan hit the button to unlock it and it beeped. Opening the door, he slid inside, started the engine, and merged into traffic. Rush hour had hit, and it took longer than usual to arrive at the hotel hosting the charity dinner.

Parking the car, he ran inside, immediately searching the crowd for Claire's face. The entire town of Amorley had come tonight—or at least it looked that way. Everyone from the hospital administration, nobility, and top business leaders came out to support the hospital. Claire would be pleased.

As his eyes surveyed the room, a man behind him cleared his throat. Ethan jumped. Turning around, he met Mr. Fulton's gaze.

"You startled me." Ethan held his breath. He'd been waiting on Fulton's answer, and with his phone missing, he hadn't talked to Fulton since the meeting.

"Sorry about that, but I wanted to speak with you before the event started. Do you have a moment?" Fulton put his hands in his pants and rocked back on his heels.

Ethan skimmed the crowd once more, but not finding Claire's beautiful face, he turned his attention to Mr. Fulton. "Sure. Have you decided on the business agreement with my family?"

Fulton's gaze clouded, and his lips settled into a thin line. "I have. It concerns me that your father has found himself in this situation. I suppose the most logical decision would be to walk away from the deal. Especially considering how things transpired between you and my daughter." He sent Ethan a pointed stare.

"I'm sorry about that, sir. I never wanted to hurt anyone. I—"

Fulton raised a hand. "No need to rehash all of that. We've discussed it, and while I disagree with your decision, I have come to understand it. Besides, my daughter is beautiful and wealthy. She'll have other suitors."

Ethan nodded. "Thanks for understanding."

Fulton dipped his head. "I considered saying no for many reasons, but after a great deal of thought and discussion with my wife, I've decided to help you. I'll sign the contract and cover your father's loan in exchange for the share in his business and estate. Of course, you'll offer your expertise as needed at no charge, per our agreement. Do we have an agreement?" He raised a brow.

Ethan's shoulders relaxed, and he smiled. He shoved his arm forward to shake Mr. Fulton's hand. "It's a deal."

Mr. Fulton took Ethan's hand and pumped it a few times before releasing it.

"Thank you, sir. Thank you so much. I can't wait to tell my father—he'll be relieved and excited about the merger."

Fulton smiled. "I look out for my business and family interests, but I'm not opposed to charitable acts. Besides, once you and your fiancé marry, you'll have a connection to the Crown—which means I'll have a closer connection, too. Working in Parliament affords access to the queen, but it won't hurt to have her husband in my back pocket as well."

Ethan's smile waned a bit as he mulled over this perspective. "Uh, sir, I can't guarantee any provisions from the queen or the queen mother. I will love her and support her leadership of Amorley. Beyond that, I can't promise anything to you. That's not why you agreed to this deal, is it?"

The man placed a hand on Ethan's shoulder. "Not at all. I'm just saying it doesn't hurt to have friends in high places. Now, enjoy your evening. Tomorrow is a big day—Coronation Day."

Ethan sent him a half-smile. "Right. Big day. Thanks." He spun around and ran a hand through his hair. What had he agreed to with Mr. Fulton? Did the man have no ulterior motives? Ethan had made clear that he wouldn't be the man's political puppet. Still—" His eyes landed on Claire standing in the middle of the ballroom. She wore a sapphire blue gown that grazed the floor and her hair in a complicated knot on top of her head. Even from this distance, her blue eyes sparkled. She glowed.

He took a few steps toward her before another figure obstructed his path—his father. "Good evening. I need to talk to you, but first I—"

James Kane furrowed his brow and stepped closer. "Ethan, I hope you have good news for me. We have to tell the bank something by tomorrow morning."

Ethan nodded. His conversation with Claire would have to wait a little longer. "I do. I spoke to Fulton, and he's agreed to take over the loan in exchange for a share in the estate and business."

In an uncharacteristic show of emotion, his father wrapped him in an embrace and clapped him on the back. After several seconds he released him, and he had tears in his eyes. "Thank you. You didn't have to help us, but you did even after I behaved horribly; even after Richard mistreated you. Why did you do it?"

Ethan shrugged. "I did it because I love my family, and I love God. He asks me to forgive and show his love to others. We all need help sometimes. We all need mercy and grace. I love you, and I forgive you."

In all of Ethan's life, he'd only seen his father cry two other times—once when Ethan's grandmother died and when his favorite team lost the polo nationals. He leaned in and gave his father another hug, inhaling the scent of his brut cologne. The fragrance brought back memories of his childhood and sitting on his father's lap.

He released Ethan from the embrace and grinned. "I love you, too. I'll call the bank manager and tell him about the loan. He can email me the papers for Fulton to sign. The bank wants them returned by seven a.m. tomorrow."

"Do it. Tell Mother, too. I would find her myself and give her the good news, but I have something else pressing that needs my attention."

His father grinned and raised a brow. "It wouldn't have anything to do with a certain young lady, would it?"

Heat filled Ethan's face. His father didn't usually tease him—most of the time, he'd scowl and touch on the importance of remaining serious at all times. He must be in a great mood to joke around like this. "Uh, yes. I have to talk to Claire."

"You'd better find her. Did you see the newspaper?" his father asked.

Ethan searched the middle of the room for Claire, but she'd moved on from her previous spot. Half-paying attention to his father's question, he muttered, "Uh, no. I didn't. I've been busy, and then I lost my phone, so I haven't done anything else besides work on the merger and drive back and forth from the office to home."

His father's smile faltered. "Oh. Well, you need to talk to your fiancé. The Crown can't be happy with the picture in the paper."

Ethan's pulse quickened. "Why?" He fiddled with one of his cuff links.

"The picture showed you and Abigail Fulton looking cozy. I assume someone took it during the meeting with her and her father, so I knew there was nothing more to it. Still, I doubt your fiancé or the queen mother appreciated the appearance of it. The Crown and the hospital detest any hint of scandal."

Ethan ran a hand across his mouth, rubbing his jaw. *No. Not now. Why did this have to happen now?* He'd finally righted things with his family, and now everything between him and Claire might be ruined by another ill-timed photograph. "I'd better go. Thanks for letting me know."

His father clapped him on the back. "If you explain everything, I'm sure she'll understand."

"I'm sure she will, too." His eyes darted from one side of the room to the other, seeking out Claire's face. As panic filled his heart, Ethan's gaze landed upon her, talking in the corner of the room to the queen mother and her granny. Perfect. He could explain the situation to all of them at one time.

He weaved his way through the crowd, nodding and smiling at familiar faces but refusing to stop—a man on a mission. A minute later, he'd arrived behind her, and when she turned around, he saw it—disappointment and distrust in her eyes. He'd lost her.

"Claire, I'm sorry that I didn't get to talk to you. I meant to call you back, but then—"

The queen mother cleared her throat and took a step forward, putting herself between him and Claire. "Young man, it appears that you have contributed to a public scandal for the Crown now not once, but twice?"

He dropped his head, staring at the floor. "Well, uh, yes, I suppose it does look that way, but if you give me a chance, I—"

Granny pounced on him. "Now, listen here, you've always been a respectable, upstanding gentleman, but when a lady calls you, you return the call. That's common courtesy. What in the world were you doing having your photo taken with that girl and then refusing my granddaughter's calls? I tell you I'd have thought you were dead, or kidnapped, or lost at sea, but now, here you are, fit as a fiddle, and I don't—" Granny clutched her chest.

Claire jumped forward and placed a hand under her granny's other arm. "Are you okay?"

Granny sputtered, "I'm—I'm fine—it's my chest, it—" She didn't finish her sentence because she collapsed to the ground like a puppet who'd had its strings cut.

Claire screamed and then dropped to the floor.

Her granny's eyes remained shut and her face resembled the color of snow.

Leaning down, Claire placed her ear above

127

Granny's mouth. Her eyes flicked to the older woman's chest, watching for chest movement.

The frail woman's rib cage rose and settled slowly.

Placing two fingers on Granny's neck, Claire held her breath. "Her pulse is thready." She glanced at the queen mother. "Call an ambulance."

The queen mother stood rooted to her spot for a moment until Claire barked again, "Ambulance. Call the ambulance now before it's too late."

The urgency in Claire's voice jolted the queen mother to attention and she dashed off to find help.

Claire placed a hand on her granny's cheek and stroked it.

A gentleman nearby removed his suit jacket and handed it to her.

She rolled it up and tucked it under Granny's head. Moving closer, Claire whispered into her granny's ear, "Hold on—don't leave me. I need you. Help is on the way." Patting the woman's forehead, Claire's eyes filled with tears.

Ethan sank next to her. "Claire, what can I do? I'm—"

She whipped her head upward to meet his eyes, not moving her hand. "I think you've done enough. If you hadn't upset her like that, she might not have collapsed. I told you a long time ago I handle things myself. This is why. I can't rely on anyone else besides my granny, and now I might lose her, too." Claire stopped talking to check Granny's pulse and respirations again. "Please go." She didn't raise her head to look at him this time.

He'd lost her trust. She hadn't given him a chance to explain. He clenched his jaw, fighting back tears. "Fine." Then, Ethan Kane turned on his heel, marched out of the ballroom, and into the night.

Chapter 19

The ambulance door slammed shut, and Claire's grip tightened on the stretcher railing.

"Ma'am," the EMT raised his forehead, "are you sure you want to ride with us? Shouldn't you follow with your security detail?"

Claire lifted a hand, interrupting him, "I'm coming. Forget the security." She gazed at her granny's lifeless body, hooked to monitors and tubing. *Please be okay.* After losing her mother, a father she never met, and her canine best friend, Milo, she couldn't lose someone else.

He shook his head, but muttered, "Okay." The siren sounded overhead as the ambulance pulled into traffic.

The EMTs continued to work on her granny, placing another IV, giving her oxygen, and monitoring the EKG.

Claire's eyes darted to the rhythm on the black monitor next to her. *Third-degree heart block.*

One of the EMTs placed a transcutaneous pacer on Granny and called ahead to the hospital to inform the emergency room know about her status.

The ride to the hospital took only ten minutes, but Claire couldn't get there soon enough. *How did this happen*? She should have detected something was wrong with Granny lately. Had Granny suffered a mild heart attack weeks or months ago, and Claire been too busy to notice? If she hadn't engrossed herself in the hospital charity events and the coronation, maybe she would have seen her granny's health decline.

Claire's eyes burned, and tears spilled down her cheeks. She wiped them away with the back of her hand and gripped the railing again. The ambulance pulled into the dock and stopped. She tucked away her thoughts and focused on what mattered right now—Granny.

The EMTs opened the ambulance doors and rolled the stretcher out of it.

As soon as the second set of wheels hit the ground, Claire jumped out of the ambulance and jogged behind the stretcher.

Heading into the hospital, a flurry of staff surrounded Granny, whisking her to an open exam room down the hall.

Claire started to follow, but a physician pulled her aside.

"Ma'am, uh, I mean, Your Royal Highness, I'm aware you're a physician, but you'll have to stand over here." He directed her to the hallway outside of the exam room.

Claire pushed around him, standing on her toes to get a look at her granny. "You're right—I'm a physician, and I can help. You can't expect me to stay over here and watch. I have to do something to help."

The man stepped in front of her, blocking her vision. "Dr. Thomson." He caught her gaze and sent her a kind smile. "I understand how you feel. If it were my loved one, I'd feel the same way. However, as a fellow physician, you know we can't let you work on your family. It's against hospital policy, and it's a bad idea. Trust us, please. I promise we'll take good care of her."

She stared at him, and the sorrow of the day filled her chest. Her palms sweat, and her breathing increased. Claire closed her eyes, and the room spun. *Don't hyperventilate. Calm down.* She clenched her hands, trying to slow her respirations and focus on what the man had said. If she fainted, she'd be no assistance to her granny. After a few seconds, she opened her eyes again. "You're right."

He pointed toward the emergency department doors. "Why don't you get some fresh air? Give my team a chance to work, and I'll update you as soon as possible."

Claire cast a glance toward the exam room one more time but then nodded. Turning around, she marched toward the exit.

The glasses doors parted, and a cool breeze hit her face.

She closed her eyes again and gulped in fresh air before crumpling to the ground in a puddle of grief. Wrapping her arms around her chest, Claire rocked back and forth. She couldn't lose her granny. The woman had practically raised her—what with her mother working all the time and not having her father present. What would she do without her?

Thunder rumbled overhead, and the scent of rain filled the air. After a loud thunderclap, the skies opened, and a torrent of rain fell.

Claire didn't move. She let the downpour wash away the tears, along with her hopes and dreams for her fairytale ending. She couldn't speak old Amorley, Ethan had kept secrets from her, and Granny's life hung in the balance. No Ethan, no coronation, no Granny. How had she let everything get so out of control?

After a few minutes, a hand landed on Claire's shoulder.

She looked up, and an older gentleman in a wool three-piece suit and wire-rimmed glasses stood over her. "Miss are you alright?" he asked.

She clenched her eyes shut and answered him through sobs, "No."

"Come inside and let me get you a cup of tea. Hot tea makes everything better."

Claire nodded. "That's what my grandmother says, too. Okay, thanks." She rose slowly and let the man guide her into the ER.

As the doors parted, they walked through them, and the air conditioning blasted Claire's core. She shivered.

The gentleman glanced at her. "You're cold." He took off his jacket and wrapped it around her shoulders.

Then, he guided her to an empty chair in the small waiting area. Blue plastic chairs lined the wall, most of them filled with patients' families. The man gestured to the available seat.

Claire smiled at him and sank into the chair. "Thanks."

"I'll get the tea and be right back." He shuffled away. His spine hunched in a permanent arch forward and silver speckled his hair.

She pulled the coat tighter and trembled. Sliding one of her hands out the front of the jacket, she pushed her matted, wet hair out of her eyes. Then, she slipped her arm back inside her woolen cocoon.

The man returned with two foam cups in hand. Another seat had opened up next to Claire, so he handed her one of the cups and eased himself into the chair. "Drink up," he encouraged her.

She pressed her lips around the edge of the cup and tipped it toward her. The warm liquid soothed her soul, chasing away the chill from the rain and the air conditioner. She lifted a hand to her face and tucked a loose strand of hair behind her ear. "Thank you again. This helps."

"Good." He took a draw off his tea and then settled his gaze on her. "Who are you waiting on tonight?"

He must not have recognized her. "Oh, my granny. We were at an event, and she collapsed—third-degree heart block and who knows what else. I'm waiting for an update from her doctor."

He nodded. "Are you two close?" he raised a brow and took another drink.

"Yeah. She's the only family I have left." Not true—she still had her grandmother and Wilson, but her granny was the last vestige of her past life—the one where the Thomson girls took on the world.

"I see. I'm sorry to hear that. I'm waiting on my niece. She had a car accident, and they're doing x-rays to see if she broke her foot. Nothing too dramatic, but I'm not a big fan of hospitals."

"I understand. I'm a doctor, too, but they wouldn't let me go back with her." She stuck her hand out through the coat the man had loaned her and offered it to him. "Dr. Claire Thomson."

He took her hand in his and shook it. "Dr. Thomson? As in the future queen of Amorley?" he asked, releasing her hand.

She shrugged. "Yeah, well, I'm supposed to be crowned tomorrow, but I don't think it's going to happen."

"I didn't recognize you at first. I guess you don't expect to see royalty in the emergency department."

"That's okay." Claire pulled her eyes away and sipped on her tea.

"Why don't you think the coronation will take place tomorrow? It's on all the news channels, and the paper had a story about it today. Things sounded definite by the media's depiction."

Claire swallowed and stared at her cup. "Well, for

me to be crowned tomorrow, I have to give a speech in old Amorley dialect, which I haven't mastered—and my granny is here, and I can't leave her. As I said, I doubt the coronation will happen, which means the crown will pass to my half-brother, Eric. It will thrill Maurelle."

The man sent her a quizzical look. "Maurelle?"

"My stepmother."

"Oh, the queen. Hmm, well, I can see how that might please her. Still, it's a shame for you to give up so easily."

"Easily?" she widened her eyes. What was easy about sitting in a hospital waiting room the night before her coronation. What could she do about any of this now?

"I don't mean to sound insensitive, but from what I've read in the newspapers, you've come so far. Maybe you need help. None of us get through life alone."

Where had she heard that before? She pulled in a deep breath and exhaled. "That might be true, but where is this help to come from the night before my coronation?"

"It just so happens—"

Granny's doctor walked up, cutting off the older gentleman's response. The physician caught Claire's eye. "Dr. Thomson, could we talk?"

She rose from her seat and nodded. Following the doctor down the hallway to an empty triage station, Claire met his gaze. "Well, how is she?" Claire held her breath, waiting for his response.

His lips settled into a serious line. "She's stable and doing much better. She was in third-degree heart block, but the transcutaneous pacing worked. We need to place a permanent pacemaker. I've notified our electrophysiologist, and he's on his way to the hospital. All I need is your consent and some papers signed. Of course, there's a risk with any procedure, but she's out of the danger zone."

The air rushed from Claire's lungs. "Oh, thank you. Thank you so much." She wrapped her arms around the doctor and squeezed. Once she stepped back, his eyes widened. "Sorry about that," she apologized.

"No problem. I'm glad I could help her. It will be a few hours until she's finished with the procedure, so I'd like to keep her overnight for observation. Is that alright?"

"Absolutely."

He clasped his hands together behind his back and dipped his head. "Great. Well, then, why don't you get comfortable in the waiting room, and once she's in a room upstairs, I'll let you know."

"Wonderful—and thanks again." She raised a hand. "I won't hug you this time. Promise."

The doctor gave her a small smile and led the way back to the hallway. He turned and headed in the direction of the exam rooms.

Claire went left, joining her mystery friend in the waiting room. She took her seat next to the older gentleman, placed both hands on her face, and sighed.

Granny was going to be okay.

"How's your granny?" the gentleman asked, still sipping his tea, jacket-less.

She'd forgotten she still wore his blazer. "Oh, I'm sorry. I ran off with this." She slunk out of it and handed it to him, still balancing her cup with one hand.

"Not a problem." He took it and raised a brow. "Your granny?"

"Oh, she's going to be alright. She has to have a procedure done, but it's not too invasive. Still, they're keeping her overnight, so I'm staying. She's sedated right now, and I want to be there when she wakes up."

The man nodded. "Good. Then, we have plenty of time to study."

Claire lifted her forehead. "Study? Study what?" She took a sip of her now-tepid tea.

"Old Amorley dialect, of course." He extended his hand. "I didn't make a formal introduction of myself. Henry Dunmore, Professor of ancient languages at Oxmund University."

No way. She shook his hand again. "You're going to teach me all I need to know for this speech by tomorrow? Is that possible?"

He released her hand and glanced at his wristwatch. "My dear, not only is it possible, it's probable—not easy, though, so we'd better start. Let me find some paper and a pen. Oh, and something hard to write on—we can't have your speech resemble a scribbled mess. That won't do." The man rose from his seat and shuffled away in search of school supplies.

Claire smiled. *God, you do know how to surprise me, don't you?*

When he returned, he carried white paper, pens, sticky notes, and another cup of steaming hot liquid.

Claire grinned. "More tea?"

He handed it to her. "It's for you. I thought a little extra caffeine couldn't hurt."

"You know, I'm more of a coffee person, but living in Amorley has started to change my mind." She took a sip. "This tea is good. Thanks."

"You're welcome—and if you're going to be queen, you have to like tea more than coffee. It's a rule."

She laughed. "You're right. Okay, so where do we begin?"

The gentleman took his seat and placed his supplies in an empty chair next to him. He turned to face Claire and pushed his glasses further up his nose with one finger. "How's your pronunciation?"

She shrugged.

"Hmm. Well, let's start there." The professor made her say the old Amorley alphabet, gave her a mini-lecture on the importance of linguistics, and wrote out word-for-word phonetically her entire speech. Hours later, fatigue and stress washed over Claire.

Claire stretched her arms overhead and yawned. "I can't believe we got through all of that. Do you think I'm ready for tonight?"

The professor removed his glasses and rubbed his

eyes before replacing the spectacles. "You're ready. Remember to take your time and bring your notes in your purse. Have them with you, just in case. Right before you go up to give your speech and accept the Crown, read them once more. Then, say a prayer and leave the rest in God's hands."

Clasping the professor's hands, Claire leaned forward. "Thank you. I couldn't have done it without you. I—"

Her granny's doctor entered the waiting room and walked toward her. "Dr. Thomson, could I have a word with you?" He tilted his head in the direction of the nurse's triage station where they'd spoken before. His mouth settled in a grim line.

Claire glanced at the professor. "I'll be right back." Then, she rose from her seat and followed the physician down the hallway. Her heart rate ticked upward, and she said a silent prayer for a good report on Granny.

Once alone, he shoved his hands in his scrub pockets and lifted his head to meet her gaze. "I have good news." His mouth cracked into a slight grin.

Claire's hand flew to her chest, and a whoosh of air left her lungs. "Oh, I thought you were going to tell me she'd a complication or something else awful had happened. You looked so serious."

He shook his head. "It's been a long night. I lost a young lady in an unexpected motor vehicle accident. Anyways, your granny is doing well. She's resting, and they moved her upstairs to a monitored bed. If her labs and EKG look good in the morning and there aren't any other surprises, then she can go home tomorrow. The pacemaker placement went well. Make her rest when she gets home, though. It may take some time for her to feel one hundred percent."

Claire nodded. "Thank you. I promise to take good care of her. She'll be mad that she can't attend the coronation, though."

The doctor's pager went off, and he pulled it out of his white coat pocket. "I have to go, but before I leave, do you have any other questions?"

Granny had made it—that was all that mattered. "No. Thank you again. I'll tell my friend goodbye and head upstairs to check on her."

Granny's doctor gave a slight bow. "Have a good day." Then, he dashed away.

Claire headed in the direction of the waiting room to say farewell to the professor and thank him for all he'd done to help her. When she arrived at their seats, only a stack of her notes, pens, and blank sticky notes remained. His cup, wool jacket, and discarded trash had vanished.

She scanned the room and hallway—no professor. He'd left. Claire scooped up her supplies, and doubt crept in about her ability to pull off the speech.

Her eyes darted to the scribbled notes on the top paper. Her loopy handwriting covered most of the page, but at the bottom, she saw unfamiliar writing—it belonged to the professor.

Glancing at it again, Claire paused. It was a verse.

"I am the vine; you are the branches. If a man remains in me and I in him, he will bear much fruit; apart from me, you can do nothing. John 15:5." Then, he wrote, "Find your help in God and those he puts in your path. I hope the coronation goes great. Your friend and loyal subject, Professor Dunmore."

Claire whispered, "Thank you for helping me, professor. I pray your niece is healed and well." Then, she dashed toward the elevator. Two minutes and several stops later, Claire arrived on her granny's floor.

Surveying the floor, Claire hunted for a glimpse of her granny. She walked to the nursing station and waited for the dark-haired nurse on the phone to finish her conversation.

Once the nurse hung up, she raised her head and asked, "How can I help you?"

Claire folded her hands on top of the counter and leaned closer. "I'm looking for someone. Her name—"

"Now, get your hands off me. I am fine. I don't know what all this hoopla is about, but it's nonsense if you ask me. Nonsense."

Granny. Claire turned her head in the direction of the unmistakable voice. She looked at the nurse again. "Never mind. I found her." She hurried to the room three doors down and knocked on the partially-closed door.

"Go away. I'm tired of being held, hostage. I don't want anyone else poking and prodding me today. Do you hear me?" Granny's weaker but still spunky voice resonated from the other side of the door.

Claire pushed the door open further. "Hey, it's me." She raised both hands in the air. "I promise not to poke or prod you."

Tears filled her granny's eyes. "Oh, my girl. Get over here and hug me." She extended her arms, draped with tape and tubing.

Claire rushed over and wrapped her arms around the woman who had helped raise her. She buried her head into her granny's neck and inhaled the faint scent of apple and jasmine from her granny's perfume. "I could have lost you," she croaked.

"Pshaw. Never. I'm too tough to put down." She patted Claire's back and whispered, "Never."

Releasing her granny, Claire sat down on the bed, taking care not to tug any of the cords and tubes. "How do you feel?"

"Like I got electrocuted. Which isn't too far off base, from what the doctor told me." Granny smoothed the white knit blanket draped across her with her bruised hands.

"Yeah, pretty much. You underwent transcutaneous pacing. Thankfully, you were unconscious for that— then they put in the pacemaker. That's a lot for one day." Claire picked at a piece of lint on the blanket.

Granny placed a hand on top of Claire's. "More importantly, how are you?"

Claire shrugged and sent her granny a smile. "I'm too tough to put down that easily."

Granny cackled. "Touché." She glanced out the

window and gasped. "It's morning. I didn't realize—the coronation."

Squeezing her granny's hand, Claire scooted closer. "Don't worry about it. That's not what's important right now."

"What are you going to do? You haven't had any sleep, have you? What about your speech? You didn't get to practice, and I heard your pronunciation yesterday—no offense, but it sounded awful."

Claire laughed. "Thanks a lot—and you're right—I didn't get any sleep, but I did meet a friend. He taught me about the importance of accepting help—from God, family, and friends."

Granny narrowed her eyes. "Exactly what kind of friend was this?"

"Dunmore. Professor Dunmore. He teaches ancient languages or something like that at Oxmund University. Last night, he spent hours helping me learn old Amorley and work on my speech. I'm ready. I hope."

Claire's granny clapped her hands. "Well, good for you! Okay, so what's the plan for today? Did Ethan come to his senses? Did you figure out what to do about the gown?"

Ethan. The dress. She'd forgotten about that—not to mention the disaster of a charity event she'd left behind.

Claire shook her head. Her eyes stung from fresh, hot tears. "Ethan doesn't want—"

"You to face all of this alone. He doesn't want you

to give up on him because he loves you. All of this was a horrible misunderstanding," Ethan's voice came from the doorway.

Lifting her head, Claire looked in his direction.

He stood against the doorframe holding a cup with steam wafting from the top of it.

She raised her brow. "What are you doing here?"

"I came to see you and check on Granny. I called the hospital last night, but they wouldn't tell me anything. I drove over her three times and turned around because I didn't want to upset you, but I couldn't stay away. Claire, everything got twisted, and it looks bad— I realize that. Nothing happened between me and Abigail, and nothing will ever happen. I love you. I shouldn't have kept the secret about my family's financial problems from you. I wanted to fix things first, handle them myself, then tell you and everyone else. I'm always the one telling you to take people's help, and I didn't follow my advice. Will you forgive me?"

Her eyes took in all of him. He wore a rumpled white dress shirt, unbuttoned at the top, and wrinkled black pants, but he still looked like the most handsome man she'd ever seen. His red-rimmed eyes exuded kindness. Ethan ran a hand through his hair and shifted his gaze to the floor.

Claire rose from the bed and walked slowly to the door. She stopped in front of him and placed a hand against his cheek.

He lifted his head and locked eyes with her. His

voice cracked, "I'm sorry, Claire. I'm so, so sorry."

"I forgive you," she whispered. "I love you, too."

Granny piped in, "Oh, go ahead and kiss her already. What are you waiting on, an engraved invitation?"

He flashed Granny a smile and looked deep into Claire's eyes. "She's right, you know. I love you, and I can't wait to see you crowned queen today. I want to marry you and start our lives together. I promise to always stand by your side and help you. Always. Dr. Claire Thomson, will you do me the honor of letting me escort you to the coronation tonight?"

Claire nodded. "I'd love to go with you." She wrapped her arms around the back of his neck and raised her head.

Ethan dipped his head lower and brushed his lips against hers. When pulled away, he grinned. "We'd better hurry if you're going to make it to the coronation on time. The two of us look like," he peered down at his clothes, "a spectacle. The queen mother won't be pleased if we show up like this."

Claire frowned. "You're right. I don't have a dress, though."

Ethan placed a strand of her hair behind her ear. "Yes, you do."

"What do you mean?" she asked.

Claire frowned. "What gown?"

He raised a finger and stepped into the hallway. Seconds later he'd returned with a garment bag.

Unzipping it, Ethan revealed a dazzling smile and Claire's grandmother's gown. "Your grandmother's gown—the one that got ruined. I wanted it to be a surprise for you. I had planned to give it to you this morning. I spoke with Mademoiselle Couture earlier this week and begged her to try one last time to fix it. Somehow, she managed. You can't tell that anything ever happened to it."

Claire's mouth fell. She reached forward and brushed her fingers along the blue and gold embroidered bodice. Inspecting the skirt for any signs of rips, stains, or loose threads, she exhaled. It looked brand new. Well, as brand new something about a hundred years old could look. "It's amazing." She lifted her eyes to Ethan's.

He caressed her cheek and leaned in once more, placing a soft kiss on her lips.

As she pulled away, she whispered, "Thank you—for everything."

He smiled and shrugged. "Of course."

Granny called from the bed, "You two better bust me out of here and get a move on it, or you're going to miss your coronation."

Ethan laughed. "She's right."

"Okay, let me find someone to release Granny." Claire started down the hall toward the nursing station but stopped and turned around. "I forgot that I don't have a car. I rode over here in the ambulance with Granny. Can you give us a ride back to the castle?"

"You got it." Ethan winked.

She flashed him a smile and resumed her mission. She could do it with God's help. Claire would take Granny home, shower, change into her grandmother's heirloom gown, and assume the throne as the next queen of Amorley.

~

Ethan dropped off Claire and Granny at the castle two hours later and helped Granny up the front steps.

She swatted at his arm as she climbed each step one at a time. "Leave me alone. I can do it. I'm not dead yet. You two act like I'm going to break. I've still got lots of horsepower left in this engine. Now hurry."

Claire flanked her granny's other side and looked over the top of her head, meeting Ethan's eyes. "I guess she's feeling better, huh?"

Ethan chuckled, hovering his hand near Granny's elbow in case she stumbled. "I'd say so."

Once inside the castle, Ethan kissed and hugged Claire and said goodbye to Granny. "I'll come back and pick you up in three hours. That should give you plenty of time to get ready and for us to make it through traffic to the Abby."

Claire waved to him. "That sounds good. Be safe."

He bounded down the steps and into his car. Then, he tore off down the road kicking up a thin cloud of dust in his wake.

Claire took her granny's arm and guided her to the stairs. "I understand you don't want help, but you're getting it."

Granny placed a frail hand on her granddaughter's. "Do you mind parking me in the parlor? I want to rest in the sunshine. She remained silent for several seconds as they walked. Patting Claire's hand, Granny raised a brow. "I wanted to ask you something."

Claire smiled. "Sure, anything."

Her granny opened her mouth and closed it. She made another attempt before finally asking, "Would I disappoint you if I didn't attend the coronation? I hate to miss such an important event and I act tough, which I am, don't you forget that, but—"

"You're wiped out after yesterday and last night. Of course, that's fine. I'd feel better if you stayed here and relaxed. Promise me one thing, though." Claire grinned.

"What's that?" her granny arched a brow. Her face looked pale without her standard fare of rouge and orangey-red lipstick.

Claire furrowed her brow. "Stay out of trouble. No schemes with Albert, no run-ins with Maurelle, no more trips to the hospital. Deal?"

Granny shoved her thin hand in Claire's and shook it. "Deal."

Nodding, Claire squeezed her granny's hand. Then, she took her to the parlor and made her comfortable on the sofa. Once Granny had settled into a cozy corner of the couch, Claire hurried out of the room.

Taking the stairs two at a time, Claire's hands shook. The day had come—Coronation Day. In less than twenty-four hours, she'd hold the title of queen of

Amorley.

She dashed down the hallway, carrying her grandmother's dress in one hand, trying not to step on it. Opening her bedroom door, Claire expected Maurelle to jump out from the other side and yell, "Boo." A silly notion, but still, Claire wouldn't put anything past her stepmother.

Chuckling at the image, Claire opened the door and winced. No Maurelle. A sigh escaped her lips, and she walked inside, closing the door behind her.

For once, Wilson napped in the corner of the room on his dog bed rather than tearing up her clothing or terrorizing the staff. His legs quivered as if chasing a rabbit or some other quick-moving mammal.

Claire smiled and headed toward the bathroom. She jumped in the shower and let the hot water wash away the stress and anxiety of the past week. Thinking about the hospital charity event, Claire said a grateful prayer for her granny's recovery and her own reconciliation with Ethan. Now, she only had to survive the coronation and her old Amorley speech, and then she could focus on her future with Ethan and their wedding.

Claire twisted the knob off as the water turned cold and reached for a towel outside the door. She pulled it off the rack and wrapped it around herself. Padding to the bathroom counter, she wiped away the fog that the shower steam had created.

Staring at her reflection, Claire swallowed. Doubt crept into her mind. Claire shook her head. No. She could do this. With the help of her fiancé, her grandmother, and God, she'd survive the speech. Right?

Claire put on her makeup, dried her hair, and slipped into her undergarments. Then, she walked to her closet, where she'd left her grandmother's dress for safe-keeping. Even though he still lay in the corner sleeping, Wilson couldn't be trusted—the rascal.

She opened the closet door and inspected the dress. *Perfect*. Removing it from the hanger, Claire slipped into the gown, and this time she didn't topple to the floor. Once in the dress, she reached her arms behind herself, tugging at the zipper. It made it halfway to its destination, and then her flexibility gave out on her. Sweating and puffing, Claire spun in a half-circle, as if the other side of the bedroom might offer increased acrobatic skills enabling her to complete the zipper's trek to the top. Nope. "Argh."

"Need help?" her grandmother's serious voice wafted through the doorway.

Claire lifted her head, and her cheeks warmed. "Sorry, I didn't see you there."

Her grandmother smiled. "I didn't mean to startle you. I was admiring my gown on you. You're lovely in it, and it looks brand new. Did Mademoiselle Couture have it cleaned?"

Claire sent the queen mother a half-smile. "Something like that. Can you zip me? I thought I could do it—back in high school, it wouldn't have been a problem—but my arms don't bend like that anymore."

Her grandmother nodded. "All you have to do is ask for my help. I'm happy to oblige." She crossed the room and joined her granddaughter. "Spin around and face the window."

Claire obeyed and spun around again.

The queen mother pulled the two sides of fabric closer together and then lifted the zipper the remainder of the way to the top. "It's perfect. Turn around. I want to see the front of it."

Again, Claire rotated, smoothing out the front of the skirt. The silk frock had an ivory background with gold and sapphire appliqué and embroidery throughout the top, trailing just below the waist. The close-fitting bodice cinched in at the waist before the skirt fanned out in a ball gown silhouette. Claire stepped into her ivory heels and waited for her grandmother's assessment.

The queen mother tipped her head to one side, taking in the entire ensemble. "Almost. Check your desk."

Claire walked to her desk, noticed a box sitting in the center. She lifted the lid, and a shimmering tiara sat on a bed of blue velvet. She gasped. "It's lovely."

"Thank you. It was one of my favorites, and I'd hoped you would wear it today. Of course, they will place the official Amorley crown on you at the church. Still, I can't have a princess wandering around an important event without a tiara."

Claire met her grandmother's eyes and saw tears in them. "Thank you. Can you help me?"

Her grandmother nodded and joined her at the desk. She pulled the sparkling jewelry out of the box and placed it on Claire's hair, careful not to disturb her chignon. "I'm not going to pin it because you'll have to remove it quickly at the coronation. As long as you don't dive off the stage and perform another medical miracle, I think it will work." Her grandmother sent her a sidelong stare.

Claire raised her hand in an oath. "I promise—no stage-diving today—on my honor."

Her grandmother chuckled. "Good. Well, we should probably leave. I'm sorry your granny will miss this."

Gathering up her purse and the notes for her speech, Claire followed the queen mother out of the bedroom. She shut the door behind with care so as not to disturb her puppy. "I know, but she needs the rest, and I told her you'd take lots of pictures with my phone." She caught her grandmother's gaze.

The queen mother's eyes widened, and her mouth dropped open at the mention of using a smartphone.

Claire laughed. "I'm kidding, but she understands. After all, the coronation is televised, so Granny can watch it live, and we can give her the details later. I told her the most important thing is that she rests to live to nag another day. She liked that idea."

The queen mother sent Claire a small smile. "Good." Heading downstairs, she led the way out the castle's front door to the black limousine waiting below.

"Grandmother, I forgot—Ethan's coming to get

me."

Her grandmother frowned. "I'm afraid we have to leave now. The abbey minister wants to meet with us a few hours before the coronation starts."

Claire rubbed a hand across her forehead. "It's fine. I'll call Ethan and tell him." She dug through her purse and pulled out her phone. Scrolling through the contact list, she pressed the button next to his name and waited as the phone rang.

A few seconds later, Ethan's voicemail answered with his standard greeting and then beeped.

"Ethan, hey, it's me. I'm going with my grandmother to the coronation. I'm sorry—I didn't know we had to arrive early. I'll meet you there. Love you. See you soon. Bye." She pressed the end button and returned her phone to the purse.

Her grandmother raised a brow. "Ready?"

Claire straightened her posture and pulled in a deep breath. "Yeah."

The queen mother slid into the backseat, crossing her feet primly.

Claire ducked her head and took the space next to her grandmother, careful not to tear the skirt of her gown. Once inside, she smoothed out her dress and placed her purse at her side. Under her breath, she muttered, "As ready as possible." The limousine left, carrying Claire away from her past and toward her future as queen of Amorley.

Chapter 20

Ethan drove to Evercliff Castle and stopped at the front. He opened the car door and placed one foot outside.

Albert stood by the side of Ethan's car, ready to assist with the door.

"Good afternoon. How are you?" Ethan greeted him.

Albert leaned forward. "I'm well. Are you here for Her Royal Highness?"

Still seated in the car, Ethan raised his gaze to meet Albert's. "Yes. Is she running late?"

Albert frowned. "Didn't she tell you? The queen mother and Claire left about forty-five minutes ago for the abbey. The queen mother informed me that the minister requested they come early. I suppose there will be a media circus, so it's just as well."

Ethan's stomach dropped. He'd missed her. Even though they'd worked things out earlier, he wanted to escort her to the coronation. It was an important day, and he wanted to support her and stand by her side. "Oh, I see. Well, maybe I can make up some time on the highway. Perhaps I won't be too late. Thanks, Albert."

The gentleman gave a slight bow. "My pleasure. Do not hesitate to let me know if I may be of any further assistance."

Ethan tucked his foot inside the car and nodded.

Albert shut the door for him and tipped his head.

Placing the key in the ignition, Ethan started the car. He pulled away in a hurry, accidentally screeching the tires with his departure.

~

The limousine thudded forward. Claire hit the side of her forehead on the window. "Ouch!" She rubbed it and then looked at her hand. *No blood, so that's good.*

Glancing out the window, Claire sighed. Horns around them honked, and one gentleman stuck his head outside of his car window, yelling either offenses or encouragement to the royal limousine. She didn't want to know which one. Turning to her grandmother, Claire asked, "Are you hurt?"

The queen mother's face had paled, and her hands trembled on her thighs, but she gave a slight shake of the head.

Pressing the button that lowered the window separating them from the driver, Claire leaned forward. "What happened?"

The driver's hands clung to the steering wheel so tightly his knuckles had turned white. He turned his head. "Someone hit us from behind. I'll call the police. Are either of you injured?"

Claire pressed her hand to her head again. "No, not really. I got a bump on the head, but it's not bad." She looked at her grandmother. "Are you alright?"

Her grandmother nodded. "Fine."

Claire addressed the chauffer again, "The queen mother is okay, too."

The driver picked up his phone. "Good. Give me a moment while I alert the authorities, and then I'll step outside and see what happened." He dialed the emergency number and spoke to an operator on the phone, giving their location and circumstances. After he hung up, he exited the car and walked behind it to survey the damage.

Claire scooted closer to her grandmother and the side of the car closest to where the driver stood. She watched as he spoke with a gentleman standing beside a massive truck. The guy looked shaken but talked and walked. Then, the limo driver walked to the front of the limousine and surveyed the scene. He picked up his pace and jogged to the car ahead.

When the truck struck them from behind, they'd hit the car in front of them, too. Had someone in the car ahead of them been injured? Was that why he'd ran ahead? Just as Claire placed her hand on the door to find out for herself, the driver returned to the limousine.

He took his seat and shut the door. Twisting around, he placed his arm on the armrest and looked at them.

"Well, the truck behind us hit our rear hard, and that sent us into the car in front of us. There's a good amount of damage to all three vehicles, but the truck driver is fine. There's an elderly gentleman in the car in front. He's talking but not making a lot of sense. A nurse that was in the car ahead of him is sitting with him."

Her grandmother snapped out of her dazed state. "Is traffic moving at all?"

The driver tilled his head to the side to meet her gaze. "I'm afraid not. It looks like the pile-up has brought everything to a halt."

An ambulance flew past their car, its sirens blaring and lights flashing.

Claire's eyes darted to her grandmother's. "Um—"

Her grandmother sent her a warning look. "Please don't."

Claire raised her forehead. "What? You don't even know what I was going to say."

The queen mother raised a hand. "I can guess. You want to help. Someone might need you. Your first duty is to patients. Am I close?"

Claire's face warmed. "Maybe—I'll go see if anyone needs help. A quick peek—that's all. If it looks like everything is under control, I'll come straight back."

Her grandmother's brow pulled downward. "I'm concerned about the well-being of the other passengers, too, but we're going to be late. I don't want to worry you, but if you aren't crowned by three p.m., then Eric takes the throne. We're running out of time. I don't mean to sound insensitive, but now that we're stuck here, and this wreck—what will we do?"

"I don't know, but I'll think of something. I promise. Ten minutes. I'll be right back." She hopped out of the car before her grandmother could object further and scampered down the road as fast as possible in three-inch heels.

As Claire approached the wreckage, she gasped. When the truck struck the limousine, the force of that collision caused the limo to crumple the rear of the car ahead of them. Lifting her eyes, the truck driver still stood outside his vehicle, his eyes wide but appearing stable otherwise.

Returning her attention to the first car, Claire walked around to the driver's side window. She bent down and rested her hands on the open window's ledge. "Hello, I'm Dr. Claire Thomson. Do you need any help?"

An older man wearing a tweed jacket and wire-rim glasses raised his head.

Claire's hand flew to her mouth. "Professor Dunmore. Oh my—are you hurt?"

The professor frowned. "Do I know you?"

He might have a concussion. Maybe worse. "You do. We met at the hospital yesterday. You taught me old Amorley for my speech tonight and gave me encouragement. You don't remember me?"

"I don't—I don't know. It's been a rough time. My niece died last night. I forget what the doctors said happened. Simple procedure. Hurt foot." He winced and rubbed the front of his head.

Claire leaned closer. "Do you know what day it is?"

He shook his head.

"What season is it?"

The man considered her question and looked around them before answering, "I don't know."

"Where do you live?" she asked.

"I can't recall. I'm sorry. I don't know what's wrong with me."

Okay, he needed to get in that ambulance pronto. Claire placed a hand on his shoulder. "Don't worry. Help is here. Wait one minute." Then, she rushed ahead to where the ambulance had parked. The EMTs had already opened the rear door and unloaded a stretcher.

She gestured with her thumb over her shoulder. "There's a gentleman in that car who may have a head injury. He's confused and having trouble with memory. I'm a physician, and I met him the other day, but he doesn't remember me."

The younger EMT clicked the second set of wheels into place and pushed the stretcher in the direction of the professor. "Thanks. We'll take it from here."

Claire stepped aside and watched as they wheeled the empty stretcher away.

The two EMTs placed a cervical collar on the professor and stabilized his spine. Then, they lifted him out of his car and put him on the stretcher. As they wheeled him past her, ready to load him in the ambulance, he shouted, "Wait."

The two EMTs paused. "What is it?" the one Claire had talked to asked.

With his head strapped to the backboard, the professor couldn't meet her gaze, but he shouted again, "I do remember you. I'll be praying for your speech. You're going to become queen of Amorley and help its people."

Claire jumped into action. "I'm coming with you. After all, you did for me; I can't send you to the hospital alone. Especially after losing your niece."

For a man strapped to a stretcher, he produced a robust response, "No. You have a duty to your country to stand in that abbey today, give your speech, and take the Throne. If you don't make it, then someone else will claim your place. No one else can do the job as well as you. Continue to show kindness to your people and let others help you, too."

Claire stood motionless.

The EMTs lifted the stretcher into the ambulance and closed one of the doors.

As the first EMT started to shut the second one, Claire shouted to the professor, "Thank you. Thank you for everything. I'll be praying for you, too."

The ambulance doors locked, and the EMT driver took his place in the front seat. The sirens sounded again, and the ambulance sped away to the hospital.

Claire stared after it for a few seconds before turning around and returning to the limousine. She opened the door and slid inside, a little less careful of her skirt this time. *What was the point? How would she make it to the abbey on time?* She wished she'd hopped in the back of the ambulance with the professor, but he was right— Claire had a duty to fulfill if she could get there.

"Well, is everything okay?" her grandmother asked.

Claire scooted closer to her grandmother. "Yes. No. I don't know. The man in the car in front of us was a friend of mine."

The queen mother adjusted her glasses on her nose. "Oh no. I'm sorry. Is he going to be fine?"

Claire wrung her hands together. "I'm praying so. He's stable for now. At first, he couldn't remember simple things, but he came around at the end. Hopefully, it's not a bleed. As soon as the coronation is over, I'm heading to the hospital to check on him."

Her grandmother frowned. "Yes, about the coronation. We still have the problem of making it to the abbey."

Claire moved over to her side of the backseat and pressed the button to lower her window. Sticking her head out, she looked to see if things had started to move.

Her grandmother called, "Anything?"

"No. It doesn't look good." Claire ducked her head inside but left the window down. "I don't know, maybe we could—"

A man wearing a suit arrived next to Claire's window. "Maybe a dashing gentleman could rescue you."

Claire couldn't see his face. "Listen, thanks for your

offer, but nothing is moving on the highway, so unless you have an airplane or a miracle, you can't help."

The man bent down and smiled. "I happen to have a motorcycle, as does my friend, Michael. Not the ideal form of transportation when wearing a ball gown, but given the current situation, it will have to do."

Claire grinned. "Ethan. How did you—when did you—how did you get here?" She leaned forward and gave him a quick kiss on the lips.

He shrugged. "I came to Evercliff to pick you up, and Albert told me you'd left. I took off to catch up with you, and on my way here, I heard about a wreck on the highway. It worried me that you might have been involved. I figured if not, I'd need the motorcycle to get you to the coronation. I detoured to Michael's and borrowed his bike. It was the only way. Albert said you were with your grandmother, so Michael agreed to come support me."

Michael dropped down in front of the window. "Hello, Claire. Quite a day, huh?"

Claire grinned. "You could say that."

Michael wore a navy-blue suit and a half-grin. He looked at the queen mother. "Are you ready to go for a ride?"

Claire glanced at her grandmother and chuckled. Her grandmother's lips pressed into a thin line, and displeasure oozed from her eyes.

"Yeah, are you ready for a ride?"

Claire smirked. *No way her grandmother would*

climb on the back of a motorcycle. No way.

The queen mother folded her hands in her lap. "Well, I suppose I don't have a choice, do I?"

Claire placed a hand on top of her grandmother's and squeezed it. "Nope. You don't. Besides, there's a first time for everything. Let's go."

Ethan stood and opened Claire's door.

Claire thanked the limo driver and told him she had to go.

He tossed her a puzzled look. She slid out of the seat and took Ethan's hand.

Ethan scooped her into his arms and hugged her tight. He whispered in her ear, "I'm glad you're okay. If something had happened to you, I—"

Claire turned her face toward his. "I'm fine, and I love you. Thank you for coming to our rescue today."

Ethan grinned. "Any time." He lowered his head and brushed his lips against hers.

Claire's pulse quickened, and she lost herself in his embrace.

"Ahem." The queen mother's voice called from behind the couple.

Claire pulled away and turned around. "Sorry."

Her grandmother adjusted her purse and stood straighter. "I don't mean to break up this lovely reunion, but we are running short on time."

Claire nodded. "You're right. I'll go with Ethan, and you can ride with Michael."

The queen mother gave a slight nod and followed

Michael to his bike.

Under her breath, Clair muttered, "I can't believe the queen mother of Amorley agreed to ride on a motorcycle."

Ethan chuckled. "Neither can I. Come on." He waved her over to his bike, tossed her a smile, and then paused. "Wait, you need one of these." He handed her a helmet.

Claire stared at it. "Oh, Grandmother will love this. So much for coronation hair." She tugged it on her head and hooked the strap under her chin.

She took her seat behind Ethan. Wrapping her arms around his broad chest, Claire rested her cheek against his back and let herself melt in the security of his strength. "Okay, I'm ready. Let's go."

Ethan started the bike and took off down the edge of the road.

Chapter 21

Ethan pulled his motorcycle up to the front of the church and killed the engine. The building had endured like a fortress for hundreds of years. It boasted a formidable wooden door that stood over three times Ethan's height. A light breeze blew, carrying with it the fragrance of honeysuckle and lavender.

He placed one foot on the ground to steady them and secured the bike. Once he'd dismounted, Ethan extended a hand to Claire to help her exit.

She took his hand, slid off the bike and removed her helmet, letting several loose tendrils fall around her face.

Ethan pushed a lock of hair off her face and cupped her cheek in his hand. "You look so beautiful."

Claire laughed and took his hand in hers. She looked down at her wrinkled dress. "I'm a mess." She pushed the hair out of her face to no avail. "I'm going to find a bathroom and attempt to repair some of this damage. Can you make sure the queen mother makes it inside safely?"

Placing their helmets on the bike, Ethan nodded.

"I'll take care of it. Go ahead. I'll find you in a few minutes."

"Thank you. I love you." She smiled and walked toward the stairs.

"I love you, too," he called after Claire. As he watched her leave, his throat tightened. He would do anything for her. He said a quick prayer for the coronation to go well and started up the stairs, too. A figure caught his attention out of the corner of his eye. She stood on the steps near the abbey's entrance.

He turned his head, and his eyes landed on a woman dressed in a full-length sapphire gown with ebony hair. *Maurelle*.

She bent down to pick something off the concrete step.

From Ethan's vantage point, it looked like a folded piece of paper. He watched as she unfolded it and turned around, appearing to scan the surroundings for something or someone.

What or who was she looking to find?

Maurelle didn't acknowledge Ethan's presence. Instead, she refolded the papers and tucked them into her purse. Then, a wicked grin swept across her face as if painted on with a brush.

That can't be good. What had made Maurelle so happy?

She took the rest of the steps, standing a bit taller, her head held high. Her dress train slithered behind her. At the top, she joined her son, Eric. Taking hold of his arm, she whispered something in his ear.

A confused look crossed his face, but he gave a slight nod of his head and walked into the church with his mother.

What were those two up to this time? Ethan wanted to find out, but he'd promised to meet Claire inside, and she might need his help. He'd have to shelf his quest to discover the inner workings of Maurelle's mind for another time.

Ethan took the stairs two at a time and hurried through the door and down the long blue-carpeted aisle leading to the front of the church.

Scanning the room, Ethan saw Michael and the queen mother. He raised his hand to get Michael's attention.

His best friend waved back and marched over with the queen mother.

Ethan extended his arm and shook Michael's hand. "Thanks for bringing my future grandmother-in-law here in one piece."

Michael grinned and crossed his arms in front of his chest. "Was there ever any doubt? You might ride a horse better than me, but my driving skills outshine yours."

Ethan shook his head. "Another debate for another day. Right now, I'm looking for Claire. Have you seen her? She was headed to the bathroom to freshen up before meeting the minister."

The queen mother looked around the room. Her

head lifted an inch upward. "There she is near the stage. Oh, and there's the minister. I'm going to gather her and start our meeting. We only have an hour until the coronation begins. They'll open the church doors to the guests in thirty minutes. We can't be seen standing here like we're attending a barbecue when they arrive."

Ethan chuckled under his breath. "No, we wouldn't want that. Okay, tell Claire I'll take a seat in the front pew."

The queen mother patted his arm. "That's fine. However, I doubt she'll come out front once we conclude our meeting. She must enter from the church doors after all the guests and attendees take their seats and make her path down the aisle to the stage. She'll take her place on the throne, the minister will conduct a brief service, and then Claire will give her speech in old Amorley. Once that's complete, I will crown her queen of Amorley, and she will exit. As she passes your pew, you may follow behind her to leave the church."

Ethan's stomach dropped. He wouldn't see her again before the coronation and encourage her. A nagging thought tugged on his mind about Maurelle's secretive antics. "I wanted to mention something to you. Maurelle—"

The queen mother waved a hand at him. "I'm sorry, Ethan, but I must go. Don't worry about Maurelle. She knows Claire is the rightful heir to the throne, and she's only attending today because duty dictates it. She's still part of the royal family, like it or not." She turned and walked toward her granddaughter.

Ethan's eyes followed her as she left, and a hollowness filled his stomach. He hoped that the queen mother was right about Maurelle, but he doubted it.

~

Claire looked at her reflection in the bathroom mirror. She'd managed to repair most of the destruction to her chignon caused by the motorcycle helmet. Still, Claire couldn't unwrinkle her dress without a steamer or a hot shower. Why hadn't she packed an emergency kit? Had she learned nothing from the last time she'd had to speak in front of an audience as a future royal—prepare for anything. After Maurelle had unintentionally (yeah, right) locked Claire in a secret room, she'd escaped and had to make a speech accepting her birthright while covered in dust bunnies and spider webs.

Well, nothing to do about that now. Claire opened her purse and pulled out a tube of lip gloss. Smoothing it across her lips, she smiled. Good, none on her teeth. Claire placed a dab of the gloss on her cheeks and rubbed. Blush—check.

Claire returned the lip gloss to her purse and extracted a tube of mascara, which she swiped across her lashes. After putting that away, she stared at the mirror once more. She looked okay. Not pristine, but good enough. What would Mademoiselle Couture think of Claire if she could see her now?

"Oh, darling, no. You aren't going out there like that, are you?" Mademoiselle Couture's voice echoed from behind Claire.

Clarrie spun around, and her eyes widened. "What are you doing here? My grandmother didn't mention that you were coming."

"Darling, when my top client has an important day, I come. I couldn't leave you, this dress, and that makeup to your hands—no offense."

Claire smirked. "None taken."

The petite woman spread her hands wide with a flourish. "Here I am—at your service. Now, let me see what we must repair. Hmm. Turn around." She made a twirling motion with one finger.

Afraid not to oblige, Claire rotated in a circle, careful not to fall this time.

The woman tilted her head and placed a hand under her chin. "Fortunately, I always come equipped." She reached in an oversized leather duffle bag that probably cost more than Claire's first apartment and pulled out a hand steamer. Then, she plugged it in an outlet near the sink and got to work. "Hold still."

Mademoiselle Couture made even strokes up and down the skirt of Claire's gown until no wrinkles remained. Then, she took Claire's hair down and reassembled the chignon. "What happened to your tiara?"

Claire's cheeks warmed. "I had to leave it in the limousine."

The woman shrugged. "Then go get it. You can't go out there with your head unadorned."

Chewing on her lower lip, Claire answered, "Well, uh, I can't. I sort of rode over here on a motorcycle."

The color drained from Mademoiselle Couture's face. "No."

Claire shrugged. "Yes. I had to do it. I didn't have another choice."

After drawing a deep breath in and releasing it, Mademoiselle Couture calmed herself. She dug around in her large bag again and pulled out a shiny object. "Aha! My staffers said I was crazy for requesting they pack this, but here we are using it. They'll never call me cuckoo again."

Claire doubted that, but she wasn't about to say it aloud. "You brought a spare tiara."

"Yes, now hold still and let me put it in your hair." She pinned it in place and stepped back. "Perfect. I'll put some makeup on you, and you'll be ready." She narrowed her eyes and leaned closer. Swiping at Claire's cheek, she brought her finger to her nose and inhaled. "It smells like strawberries. Did you—did you use lip gloss on your face?"

Claire twittered. "Uh, desperate times and all that."

Shaking her head, Mademoiselle Couture muttered under her breath, "Of all the things I've done in my life, if I can pull this off—they don't pay me enough and someday—there, all done." She stepped back from her work and gestured with her hands like a game show assistant. "What do you think?"

Claire turned toward the mirror. Her jaw dropped.

"I look beautiful. Thank you. Thank you for your help."

For the first time, Mademoiselle Couture blushed. "It is nothing—it's my job. Now, you better go. Your grandmother was looking for you, and you only have thirty minutes until the coronation begins. Guests have already started to arrive."

Not knowing whether to shake Mademoiselle Couture's hand or hug her, Claire went for a middle-of-the-road approach and did a small curtsy. "Thanks again." Then, she pushed open the door to the bathroom and hurried down the hall to the rear of the stage in the wings so no one in the auditorium could see her.

Claire chewed her fingernail. Had she forgotten anything? She had her purse, a tiara, and a dress that didn't look like a crumpled bedsheet. What else did she need?

The queen mother appeared at Claire's side. "There you are. I've been looking for you. I feared you'd changed your mind and run away."

"No way, Grandmother. I'm ready. Mademoiselle Couture helped me touch up my hair and makeup. Where's the minister?"

The queen mother gestured toward a man standing behind Claire. "He's over there waiting on us. Let me introduce you to him. He's going to walk you through the ceremony one last time and remind you of where to stand. Of course, you'll sit on the throne at the end. He had a special podium brought onto the stage for you to stand behind when you give your speech."

Claire gasped. Her speech. "Uh, hold on one second." She glanced down at her purse and noticed the clasp hung open. It must have broken. Praying for a miracle, she dug through tubes of makeup, empty gum wrappers, and pens. No speech. Where had she put it? It was definitely in there when she was in the limousine. How could it have fallen out? What would she do?

Her grandmother frowned. "Is there a problem?"

"Um, no, yes, well, I can't find my speech. The paper with my notes on it—the ones to help me remember how to pronounce the old Amorley words—is missing. I had it in the limousine, but my purse clasp must have opened, and I guess the speech fell out of it."

The queen mother paled. She whispered, "What will you do? Can you say it from memory?"

"I don't know. Let's meet with them minister and then I'll check the bathroom and find Ethan. Maybe he has it in his pocket or something."

Her grandmother nodded.

The two women joined the minister and listened as he reviewed the order of events for the coronation. He told Claire to enter from the entrance of the church and stroll down the aisle. "Be careful not to trip on the carpeting. I hate to tell you how many times I've seen a heel snagged on it."

She found that remark funny and, under normal circumstances, would have laughed, but with the disappearance of her notes, she'd lost her sense of humor, too.

Then, he advised her to take the stairs to the stage and join him in the center. He would escort her to the throne, where she would take her seat. After he conducted his part of the ceremony (which sounded more like a Sunday morning sermon), then he'd give the floor to Claire for her speech. Finally, her grandmother would place the royal crown on her head and declare her the queen of Amorley—if she made it past the address.

Claire raised a finger. "Sir, could you give me five minutes? I need to go to the restroom."

"Of course, of course, but hurry. The coronation begins in fifteen minutes. The press is waiting and watching for any misstep, so we mustn't make one. We will begin on time."

She smiled through gritted teeth. "Right. No missteps. Got it."

Claire turned and dashed down a back hallway to the restroom where Mademoiselle Couture had helped her earlier. She pushed open the door and scanned the floor furiously for the scrap of paper that held her future. Not on the floor.

Bending down, she looked under the sink and around the trashcan. Still nothing. Could she have placed it on the windowsill? Claire walked over to it and ran her hand across the ledge. Nope. The open window invited in the sound of birds chirping and traffic on the nearby street. Claire peered outside, noticing a small pond below.

The bathroom door opened, and high heels clicked

against the marble floor. "Looking for something? Shouldn't you be with the queen mother and the minister? The coronation is about to begin."

Claire spun around. Maurelle. "I know. I lost something essential, and I thought I dropped it in here."

Maurelle sauntered closer and stopped next to the window beside Claire. She reached into her pocket and pulled out folded pieces of paper. A wicked grin tugged at her lips. "It wouldn't happen to be this, would it?"

Claire's eyes widened. Maurelle had her notes—all of them. "Where did you find that?" She pointed to the paper.

Maurelle shrugged. "Oh, walking into the abbey, I noticed these scraps of paper on the ground. They didn't look important, but I couldn't leave trash on the ground."

Claire reached her hand out with her palm open, waiting for Maurelle to return her property. "May I have it please?"

"Oh, my dear, you didn't plan on using notes to give your coronation speech, did you?" Maurelle frowned.

Claire's face burned. "Well—"

"You cannot stand before your fellow countrymen and make your first remarks as the queen of Amorley using notes. Unacceptable. Besides, you've studied for weeks. You're prepared, right?" She arched a brow.

"I did study a lot, and I've worked hard, but—"

Before Claire could complete her sentence, she watched, aghast, as Maurelle tossed the notes out the window.

Claire gasped and stuck her head out the window. They fluttered through the air to the pond two-stories below. "No. No, no, no. Please, no." She banged the windowsill with her hand. Turning to look at Maurelle, she met her gaze. "Why did you do that?"

Maurelle pressed her lips together in a thin line. "Trust me. I'm doing you a favor. You would look ridiculous standing behind a podium as the queen of Amorley reading hand-written notes from a scrap of paper. You're better than that." She pulled her eyes away and inspected her blood-red nails. "Besides, there's nothing to do about it now." Glancing at her gold wristwatch, Maurelle continued, "You should find your grandmother. The coronation begins in five minutes."

Claire's palm began to sweat. What was she going to do? She ducked her head back inside the window. "Do you mind giving me a minute to myself? I want to gather my thoughts."

Maurelle pasted a forced smile on her face. "Of course. Best wishes to you." She turned to leave but paused. "If you can't give your speech today, the country will understand. After all, no one expected a commoner to take the throne in only a few short months. Eric would gladly step in and fill the role for you. Something to consider."

Yeah, right. "Thanks, but that won't be necessary. I'll figure out something." Claire watched Maurelle's eyes flash with anger for a brief second before she recovered her austere mask.

"Hmm. We shall see." Maurelle spun around, whisking the train of her dress behind her as she exited the bathroom. The door closed behind her with a loud click.

Paranoid, Claire rushed over and twisted the handle. She didn't put it past Maurelle to lock her inside a room. Testing the doorknob, it turned quickly. *Whew*. Well, at least this time, her stepmother hadn't locked her away— she'd just thrown out Claire's hopes and dreams to serve Amorley with a toss of her hand. Claire didn't buy Maurelle's message of doing this for Claire's good, either, but she couldn't focus on how Maurelle had wronged her. Right now, she had to find Ethan. Maybe he'd have a miraculous idea.

She crossed the room and peered out the window one more time, staring at her poor, soppy notes in the pond. Could she fish them out of the water? *No, that's crazy*. She'd get soaked, and it would ruin the coronation, too. Shaking her head, Claire walked to the door, opened it, and hurried down the back hallway to find Ethan as discretely as possible. If the press caught a glimpse of her, they'd never leave her alone, and she could forget calling in the troops.

Once in a side room near the church entrance, Claire peered her head out and searched for her fiancé. She cupped her hands around her mouth and hissed, "Ethan. Ethan."

Mademoiselle Couture stood a few feet away, chatting to one of her staffers. She caught Claire's gaze and sent her a puzzled look.

Claire waved and flapped her arms in the air like an air traffic controller.

The fashion guru's face paled and she rushed toward Claire. Ducking inside the wood-paneled meeting room, she asked, "What are you doing? You look like a crazed bird flinging your arms around like that? Why are you here right now? You should be backstage with your grandmother and the minister. The press will see you. Also, why were you hissing like a goose—it's unbecoming."

Claire grabbed Mademoiselle's hands in hers. "I wasn't hissing like a goose—or maybe I was, but that's not the point. You have to find Ethan and bring him to me. It's important."

The fashionista's eyes widened at Claire's urgency and forcefulness. "Okay, I'll do it, but you must hurry. It's almost time to start. Oh, and don't do that arm-waving thing again. You will give my work a bad name."

Claire pushed her away. "Yes, yes, I know. No more arm-waving. Got it. Please go and hurry."

The petite woman left the room, closing the door behind her. Less than a minute later, she returned with Ethan in tow. "You're fiancé, per your request. Now, may I return to my staff? Even though it doesn't look like it, I'm swamped."

"Yes, of course. Thank you." Claire watched as the woman left the room for the second time.

Ethan closed the space between them and took

Claire's hands in his. "What's wrong? Mademoiselle Couture came to me and said you were having a fit. Something about you dancing around like a bird and that you'd become unhinged."

"I wasn't having a fit, and I'm not unhinged, but—" Claire pressed a hand to her chest, which had tightened. She tried to breathe, but the room spun. *Do not faint. There's no time for that.* Her medical training kicked in, and she took a seat in one of the chairs that surrounded the conference table. Leaning forward, she placed her head between her legs and drew in slow, deep breaths. After a few of those, her heart rate slowed a bit.

Ethan placed a gentle hand on her back. "Claire. Calm down. Talk to me. What happened?"

Still bent over, Claire muttered, "They're gone. Gone. She threw them away."

Rubbing her back to console her, Ethan asked, "Threw what away?"

"My notes—all of them. Maurelle tossed them out the bathroom window and into the abbey's algae-filled pond. I have nothing."

Ethan's hand stopped. "Oh, I see. You can't do the speech without the notes?"

Claire didn't answer.

He kneeled in front of Claire and rested his hands on her knees. "You can do this."

Claire lifted her head and looked into his eyes. "I don't know if I can. What if I make a fool of myself and let my father, mother, and grandmother down?"

"I know that you can do it because God has ordained you to become the next queen of Amorley. He can work out everything, even the bad things, for your good. I understand not having your notes makes you anxious, but you're brilliant. You've studied hard, and you have all that knowledge inside of you."

Claire smiled. "You think it will be okay?"

Grazing her cheek with his thumb, Ethan smiled. "I do."

His touch sent a tingle down her spine and she shivered.

Ethan leaned closer and pressed his lips against hers.

His kiss melted away her fears and concerns and her shoulders relaxed. After a few blissful seconds, she pulled her lips from his and stared into his eyes. "What do I do now?"

He stroked a loose tendril of her hair and let it fall between his fingers. "Take a deep breath."

She obeyed, inhaling and exhaling slowly. On her second round of breaths, her phone rang, jolting her out of the serene moment. Claire dug through her purse and extracted it, staring at the screen. *Oxmund Hospital. Now what?* Pressing the green button, she answered, "Hello?"

"Yes, may I speak to Dr. Claire Thomson?" a weak voice asked.

"This is her. How may I help you?" she asked. *Perhaps it was about a patient?* She'd signed out all of her cases to a colleague for the week, but maybe they needed her.

"This is Professor Dunmore. I demanded they let me call you. I wanted you to know that I'm going to be fine. Maybe not right away, but soon. The doctor in the emergency department said I had a concussion, but they are keeping me for observation."

She sighed. "That's great news."

"There's something else—with your coronation today, I'm sure you are stressed. I'm praying for you, and you're going to do great. I've never seen someone pick up an ancient language as fast as you. Do you have your notes?"

Claire's stomach clenched. "It's funny you should ask that—they've gone missing."

He went quiet for a second before responding, "No matter. You don't need the notes. You can do it."

Tears burned her eyes, and her throat tightened. "I hope so. Thank you. Thank you for your help, and for the call—I needed it. Now, you should rest. Don't worry about me."

"I will but remember—have a little faith—in yourself, in those who've helped you arrive at this point, and in God. Have a good coronation, Queen Claire. Goodbye." The line went dead.

Claire returned her phone to her purse then cast a glance at Ethan.

Ethan furrowed his brow. "Who was that?"

She grinned, wiping at the tears in her eyes that had caused her vision to blur. "Professor Dunmore—he's going to be okay. He told me to have a good coronation and said he believed in me. He said he's praying for me."

Ethan sent her a soft smile. "That was thoughtful of him." He took hold of her hands. "Okay, now close your eyes."

Claire hesitated for a second but then shut her eyes.

He cleared his throat and lowered his voice, "I'm going to pray for you, too." Ethan squeezed her hands and continued, "God, please help Claire today. Give her the confidence to stand before this crowd, knowing You appointed her for this position. Help her remember her speech and feel peace as she takes the stage. Thank you for this beautiful, smart, kind woman. May she rule over Amorley with Your love and blessing. Amen."

Claire opened her eyes and met Ethan's gaze. "Thank you for loving me and believing in me. I can do it. With God's help, I can do it."

Ethan beamed. "That's the spirit." He rose from his knee and stood straight. Then, he extended a hand to her.

She placed her hand in his and got up from her seat. Claire shook out the skirt of her dress and grabbed her purse from the table. She could do this. "I'm ready. I'd better find my grandmother. It's time."

Ethan nodded and gave her one last quick kiss. "I love you, and I'll be waiting for you when you exit."

Claire gave a slight nod and headed toward the door. She placed her hand on the doorknob and paused. A vision popped in her head of herself wading through algae to extract the notes. Turning her head to look back at Ethan, she asked, "It's too crazy to jump in the pond, right?"

Ethan laughed. "Yes. Too crazy, and not necessary."

She sighed. Muttering, she turned the knob, "That's what I thought." Then, Claire hurried down the back hallway once more to the rear of the stage.

~

"Where in the world have you been? I almost sent a search party out looking for you. The coronation begins in one minute. My heart can't tolerate this." The queen mother pinched the bridge of her nose with her fingers. "This is not how I planned this day. I'm not sure which is worse, that you haven't had a proper last-minute run-through or that I rode on the back of a motorcycle."

Claire shrugged. "Let's call it a draw."

The queen mother blew out an exasperated sigh. "Fine. Are you ready?" Her grandmother raised her forehead.

Claire's pulse quickened. A knot formed in the back of her throat, and she swallowed hard. However, instead of turning in the opposite direction and fleeing, she answered, "Yes," with as much authority as she could muster.

The minister approached Claire and guided her through a secret hallway to the entrance of the church. In an antechamber, the two of them waited until an organ played the Amorley song. He turned to her. "Are you nervous?"

Claire's palms dampened. She rubbed her hands together, careful not to let them brush against her gown. "A little." *That's an understatement.*

He nodded. "Understandable. Pay attention and you'll do fine. Don't fall and remember your speech. I'll go back the way we came and wait for you at the front."

The doors to the main hall of the abbey opened, and Claire exited, marching down the aisle alone. As she passed by rows of familiar faces, she pasted the pleasant smile on her face her grandmother had taught her. Determined not to tumble in the dress this time, Claire focused on taking careful steps as she navigated the carpet.

As she passed Ethan, he sent her a wink.

Michael gave her a small wave and a thumb's up sign.

Claire stifled a chuckle and focused her gaze forward. *Tall posture, smooth steps, head lifted.* She repeated the chant over and over until she arrived at the stage and exhaled. She'd made it.

The minister greeted her at the front and guided her up a set of stairs to the throne. Claire turned to face the audience and took her place on the gold and jeweled seat. She focused on the cool metal against her skin and took slow, steady breaths.

The minister conducted his sermon, which took thirty minutes. When he'd finished, he made a gesture toward Claire. "Now, it is time for the heir apparent to make her acceptance address for the Crown in old

Amorley."

The gentleman exited the stage, and Claire rose from the throne. She crossed the floor to stand behind the podium and her heels made a resounding echo in the room. Gripping the podium, Claire placed trembling fingers on either side of it. Her heart raced, and her palms sweat, but she pulled in a breath and released it. Opening her mouth, she spoke in old Amorley, recalling every word of each paragraph she'd practiced—without notes. Staring ahead as she made her conclusion, her eyes settled upon Ethan.

He smiled and gave her a discreet nod.

Claire grinned. "Thank you for accepting me as one of your own. I've loved spending the last several months learning about my father's country and its people. You are what makes this country so special. Although, I got off to a rocky start in my early days here, you have extended me patience and grace. I will pray daily that I may lead in a manner deserving of your trust and the honor of the title of queen of Amorley. I would not stand before you today if it were not for the help of others. To my grandmother, thank you for teaching me the importance of tradition; to my Granny, thank you for demonstrating to me the value of laughter; to my fiancé, thank you for showing me the depth of your love; and to Mademoiselle Couture, thank you for dressing me in a manner suitable for a queen. May God bless Amorley and may God bless you all."

The audience erupted in applause and cheered.

Tears sprang to Claire's eyes, but she recalled the queen mother's advice to remain poised and composed. She dipped her head and did one of her awkward curtsies before returning to the throne and taking her seat.

The crowd quieted as the queen mother entered the stage carrying the crown.

The minister followed behind her with the scepter atop a pillow.

At least Wilson wasn't here today to play fetch with the crown jewels. The thought made Claire chuckle.

Her grandmother faced Claire, her back to the audience, and sent her granddaughter a warning look.

Uh, oh. Better behave. Claire put the serene smile on her face again—the one that her grandmother deemed appropriate for public occasions and sat still.

The queen mother lifted the crown high above Claire's head and announced, "I pronounce you, Dr. Claire Thomson, daughter of Mona Thomson of the United States and Alexander Evercliff, former King of Amorley, the Queen of Amorley. Long live the queen." She placed the crown on Claire's head and turned to face the assembly.

The entire room cheered in response, "Long live the queen," and then stood, clapping at a deafening level.

Claire rose from her seat and accepted the scepter from the minister.

He gave her a slight bow and then exited the stage.

Claire walked forward and stopped in the center of the stage near the top of the stairs. The ovations in the room intensified. She smiled and gave the crowd the smallest of nods—she didn't want the crown to fall off like the last time she'd practiced. *Why couldn't they throw some hair pins in with it?*

Claire descended from the stage, taking each step with care, and Ethan fell in line behind her as she exited the church. Once outside, she made her way to an awaiting limousine. A staff member opened the door for her, and she slid inside the car.

Ethan joined her, and the staffer closed the door behind them.

A whoosh of air left Claire's lungs. "I'm so glad that's over. I thought I might trip, or fall, or pass out, but you were right—God helped me through it. No mishaps." The car pulled away, and as the crowd behind her faded, Claire looked at her fiancé. "Thank you for praying for me and for your encouragement."

Ethan beamed. "You were amazing. Simply amazing. You didn't miss a single word." He scooped her into his strong arms and pressed his lips against hers. When they parted, he leaned close to her ear and whispered, "I love you, Queen Claire. Now and forever, you have my heart."

Her throat ached. Happy tears threatened to fall this time. "I love you, too."

He gazed into her eyes before asking, "What's next for us? I reconciled with my parents—at least for now. Their business has stabilized, and mother and father are speaking to me again. Richard is, well, Richard. The queen mother crowned you the queen of Amorley, and things at the hospital and the charity seem good."

Claire glanced at their hands interlocked, and then her eyes returned to Ethan's. "There is one thing."

"What's that? Anything at all—I'm ready for it."

She stared into his eyes and smiled. "We have to plan a wedding. In less than a few months."

He shrugged. "Is that all? That's easy. We've dodged your stepmother's traps twice. You've learned an ancient language, saved a man's life at a charity event, and survived a coronation. A wedding should be a breeze."

Claire laughed. "A breeze. Right. I hope so, but no matter what happens, I can't wait to marry you, Ethan Kane."

He moved closer, his warm breath tickling her ear, "I can't wait to marry you, my queen." Ethan kissed his soon-to-be bride, and Claire's heart swelled in her chest. The future held faith, family, hope, and love—and she couldn't wait for it.

The End.

Newsletter signup:
https://www.jillboyceauthor.com/contact-1

Hook for the next book:

How will Claire handle royal life as the new queen of
Amorley while she prepares for a wedding that may not
happen? Find out what's next for Claire in the Royal
Medicine Series by staying in touch here:
www.jillboyceauthor.com

Also by Jill Boyce:

Harte Broken

About the Book:

Time doesn't heal all wounds. Love does.

Amy Harte, an Emergency Medicine physician, lost her
mother to cancer suddenly on the day of her residency
graduation one year ago. As a doctor, she struggles with
not being able to save her mother and experiencing her

best day on her worst. Since then, she has turned from her relationship with God in her guilt and grief. Near the fateful day's anniversary, her father calls to tell Amy the bank may take her childhood home. Amy knows she must save the house that holds the last precious memories of her mother.

Meanwhile, Amy meets a gorgeous Christian man, Seth, who slowly restores her belief in love and God's goodness. Their happily ever after may have to wait because Dr. Mark Blakely, Amy's dashing hospital colleague, has never met a woman he couldn't woo. Still, Amy suspects Mark values the chase more than her heart. Time is running out for Amy to save her family home and release her anger and guilt. Will she discover that love, especially God's love, heals all wounds?

Sneak Peek the First Chapter:

Psalm 147:3 He heals the brokenhearted and binds up their wounds.

Chapter 1

July 2, 2017, Sunday

Amy Harte stared at the brass nameplate in front of her as she knelt on the cool green lawn. She ran her fingers over the letters, tracing the precious name. Her gaze shifted to the tilted vase attached to her mother's headstone, and she reached out to straighten it. A light breeze blew past, carrying the sharp scent of freshly cut grass.

"I'm sorry, Mom. I'm so sorry." Only silence answered. She drew in a shuddering breath. Today marked an anniversary she never wanted to celebrate. One year ago, Amy had graduated from residency and fulfilled a lifelong dream to become a physician—but on that same day, she lost her mother. How does one celebrate when the best day of life is also the worst?

Guilt washed over Amy as she reflected on how she'd let her mother down. She'd missed being with her when she passed and still carried the burden of failure to save her mom despite being a physician tasked with healing others.

The phone call Amy had received earlier that morning from her father rose in her thoughts. "Hello," she'd mumbled.

"Amy? Did I wake you?" Her father's low-timbered voice bellowed.

"Dad, are you okay?" Amy rubbed the sleep out of her eyes and tried to gain her bearings.

"Yes," her dad's voice trailed off.

"What's going on?" The last year's events flashed through her mind, and she felt a rock developing in the pit of her stomach.

"It's about the house. I got a call Friday morning

from the bank and met with the manager."

Amy ran a hand through her hair, relaxing a bit. "Dad, you haven't had a mortgage in years."

"Well, that's true. We did pay it off a few years ago."

"Okay, so then what's the problem?"

"The problem is that because of the cost of your mom's treatments and then the funeral, I had to take out a second mortgage on the house. I didn't know what else to do…"

She frowned. "So, what does this mean? Can't we ask the bank for an extension? I'm sure they'll understand."

"They understand, but that doesn't change the fact that the bill is due. The bank manager said that I have sixty days to come up with the rest of the loan, $50,232, or the house will go to foreclosure," his voice cracked.

She could tell he was close to tears. "Oh, Dad. Don't cry. We'll figure something out." Amy wracked her brain, calculating her student loan balance, which teetered over the six-figure mark, and considered her rent and car payment. She just started working at Metropolitan
Hospital, so her savings account was anemic.

"They can't take your home." She'd had tea parties there with her mother. It was where she had learned to ride a bike and gotten ready for prom. "Where would you live?" Amy tried to conceal the rising panic in her voice.

"Don't worry about me. The money from my pension more than covers my monthly living expenses, and I'm sure I could find something reasonable to rent."

"No. Absolutely not. We lost mom. We can't lose the family home."

"Well, if you come up with a way to make fifty-grand in the next sixty days, let me know. Otherwise, I think it would be a good idea if you came over in the next few weeks to go through things."

"Don't start packing up yet, Dad. I love you." Amy hung up and made a silent vow to save her childhood home.

A butterfly landed on her hand, snapping Amy out of the memory. Hot tears stung her eyes, and a single droplet rolled down her cheek. She wiped it away and shook her head. No time for tears today. She stood and brushed tiny blades of grass off her faded mint-green scrub pants.

A grey-haired older gentleman dressed in overalls stood a few feet away, raking mulch into a flowerbed. "You've got to receive God's forgiveness sometime, young lady." He continued his work as he spoke, not lifting his head.

Amy stood straighter and pressed her lips into a firm line. "Excuse me, what did you say?"

The stranger halted his task and rested his arm on the rake. His eyes found Amy's. "I said, you're going to have to accept God's forgiveness…only way to move forward. Guilt will eat you up inside and make it hard to love and live." The man shrugged and resumed his work as if never a word was spoken.

Her mouth fell open. *What does he know about God's forgiveness? He's probably crazy.* She started to refute his intrusion, but her pager beeped, reminding her to get moving. She walked to her car and hopped inside.

The muggy summer air, combined with choking

grief, made breathing difficult. She cranked up the air conditioning and drove across town, arriving at the parking lot of Scottsburg, Virginia's community hospital. She stopped the car, stamped down the emergency brake, and paused. "Come on, Amy. Get it together. You're a professional." She slid out of the car and walked toward the hospital with hurried steps.

Straightening her shoulders, Amy stepped past the main glass doors of Metropolitan Hospital and entered the five-star, luxury-hotel-like foyer. Despite the crystal chandelier hanging overhead and a white marble floor below, the classic scent of bleach revealed it to be a well-endowed medical facility with an expansive, wealthy board of directors and donors.

Amy strode into the Emergency Department and sent a nod to her best friend and lead respiratory therapist. "Hey Beth, how's it looking today? Swamped already?"

Beth, petite with shoulder-length blond hair, leaned against the central nursing station, the main activity hub. She flicked her hand with a quick wave and grinned. "Hey, Amy!" Glancing at the large whiteboard filled with patients' names and room assignments confirmed her assessment.

Blowing her bangs out of her eyes, Beth nodded her head. "Yeah, it's been a madhouse. I thought people slept in on Sundays."

"I suppose some people use Sundays to get things done. You know… laundry, dishes, late brunches, grocery store runs… or go to church, I guess."

Some people, but not Amy. Tears threatened to spill over again, but she turned her head away and

forced them back down. She held her breath. A gentle hand settled on her arm, and
Amy met Beth's sympathetic eyes.

"Hey, do you need to go home? I know this must be a hard day for you. If you want, I can tell them you didn't feel well."

She gulped in a fresh breath of air and exhaled. Amy shook her head. "No, I'm fine." As she reached for a chart, the overhead paging system announced an incoming emergency.

An ambulance siren blared, and two EMTs burst through the ED's double doors.

Amy rushed toward them.

The first medic rattled off statistics. "Victim is Brian Broadstone, driver in a two-car motor vehicle accident. He suffered a head trauma and suspected concussion, with a laceration to the right scalp. Vitals are stable."

She shifted her eyes from the patient to the medic. "Thanks, I'll take it from here." She grabbed her stethoscope from her neck and began her exam. After finding the patient in stable condition, she sent him to get a head CT.

The emergency department double doors parted again, and a tall, handsome man with dark brown hair burst through them. His eyes widened as he saw Brian's stretcher roll away.
"Hey, where's my brother going?"

He wore a black short sleeve t-shirt stretched snugly across his broad chest and thick shoulders and flattered his fit physique. His chiseled jaw clenched, and concern clouded his chestnut eyes.

Amy's cheeks warmed, and she blinked hard.

Pay attention. She shook her head, gathering her thoughts. "Hi, I'm Dr. Amy Harte. Your brother's stable, but I sent him off for imaging. A head injury warrants a thorough workup. Were you in the car with him?" She smiled, hoping to ease his worry.

"Yeah, sorry I'm late. I rode over in the ambulance but stepped outside for a minute to call my dad. I didn't want my parents to hear about the accident from someone else."

Nodding her head, Amy understood. She knew how Scottsburg's rumor mill operated.

The handsome man met Amy's gaze, and his serious expression relaxed as he took a few steps closer. "Is he going to be okay?"

"I think he'll be fine, but I don't want to miss anything. Are you okay? We can evaluate you, too."

"I'm fine. Not a scratch on me." He stretched his hand toward Amy. "I should introduce myself. My name is Seth."

She shook his hand, and a shiver traveled down her spine at his touch. Releasing his grip, she cleared her throat. "Nice to meet you. If your brother's tests are normal, then he may be able to go home tonight as long as someone stays with him." Amy attempted to keep her tone even and professional. "Where were you guys headed so early this morning?"

The good-looking stranger grinned and shifted his weight. "Well, this week is our mother's birthday, so we were headed to grab breakfast, then take in the early church service so we'd have time to get things together afterward for her big day."

She raised her brow. "Did you make it to breakfast?"

Seth shook his head. "No, we didn't. Come to think of it, I'm starving. Do you think I have time to run to the cafeteria and grab something before Brian gets back?"

Amy smiled and nodded. "Sure. That's fine. I'll let him know where you went. If you're like me, it's hard to function before coffee."

Seth nodded. "Same." Seth searched her face, his eyes warm with interest. "Would you like a cup? I'll bring you one back."

Amy's cheeks burned, and her palms grew damp. Her fingertips tingled. She longed to say yes, but she feared that the names on the whiteboard were multiplying by the minute.

Someone tapped her on the shoulder. She turned, and Dr. Mark Blakely stood with two foam cups in hand.

Mark wore a confident grin as he eyed Seth. "No worries. I've got it covered." He passed one of the cups to Amy.

She hesitated, then accepted it. "Thanks, Mark."

Disappointment flashed across Seth's face for a moment. "Okay. Thanks again for taking great care of my brother." He smiled and reached out to shake Amy's hand again. "I'll be right back." Seth turned and walked away.

Mark left Amy's side to attend to another incoming patient.

Amy wished she could have talked to Seth longer, but Mark had impeccable timing.
Mark asked her out on a date weekly, despite her lack of encouragement. She suspected Dr.
Blakely's dating record included most of the female

population of Scottsburg.

Amy approached Beth standing at the nursing station and noticed an unmistakable smirk on her best friend's face. "So, I see you've met the new Chief Financial Officer."

Exhaling for the first time in a minute, Amy asked, "What do you mean?"

Beth's grin widened, and she crossed her arms in front of her chest. "Seth Broadstone. The charge nurse told me your patient's brother is the new CFO of the hospital. Apparently, he started a few weeks ago. So, this should be interesting. I saw the look between the two of you."
She winked.

Amy rolled her eyes. "I don't know what you're talking about...there was no look. Besides, right now, I don't have time to date anybody. I have a lot on my mind." Her thoughts drifted to the conversation she'd had with her dad about her parent's house. "I'm channeling all my energy into work." She owed it to her mom.

Beth's face fell, and she grew serious. "Hey, I get it. Your work is your life...but don't forget to make time for some fun, too. I guess we hadn't met Seth yet because he's stationed on the floor with the administrators."

Shrugging in nonchalance, Amy agreed, "You're probably right." She secretly hoped this wouldn't be the last time their paths crossed.

Author Biography:

Jill writes inspirational romantic fiction with a medical theme. Her debut novels are part of the A Dose of Love series. Each story can stand alone, but all feature strong female leads facing challenging life circumstances while finding love along the way. Jill's love of romance and her experience of losing her mother on the same day of her daughter's birth inspired the first novel, Harte Broken. It raises the question, "What happens when the best day is also the worst one?"

Royally Confused, Book One in the *Royal Medicine Series* introduces Claire Thomson, the heroine physician who must discover her worth by finding out her true identity. Jill enjoys royal romances and wanted to create a contemporary world filled with classic fairy-tale characters—a knight in shining armor, an evil Queen, and yes, a princess. Of course, Claire slays her own dragons and learns she comes from the one true King, her heavenly Father, who declares her worthy and loved. This series will follow the characters forward in the fictional royal world of Amorley.

Jill is a physician and mom, who loves coffee, travel, and anything glittered. She treasures spending time with her husband and children, who are her heart and greatest joy.

Let's stay in touch! Follow me on:

Facebook to enjoy #fun, faith, hope…and a little

coffee!

Jill Boyce, Author, LLC

Check out my **website**— www.jillboyceauthor.com to join my monthly newsletter and hear about my puppy's latest hijinks, new releases, discounts, giveaways, and other great deals!

Connect with me on **Twitter** or **Instagram** as well!

Join me on **Goodreads** and **BookBub** to find out what I'm reading!

Books By Jill Boyce

A DOSE OF LOVE SERIES

Harte Broken (Book One)

Perfectly Imperfect (Book Two

A Prescription for Beauty (Book Three)

ROYAL MEDICINE SERIES

Royally Confused (Book One)